THE UNDEAD TWENTY-SIX

RR HAYWOOD

1899 INC LTD

Copyright © 2024 by RR Haywood

All rights reserved.

No part of this book may be reproduced in any form or by any electronic or mechanical means, including information storage and retrieval systems, without written permission from the author, except for the use of brief quotations in a book review.

CONTENTS

Untitled	v
Prologue	1
Chapter 1	43
Chapter 2	63
Chapter 3	65
Chapter 4	74
Chapter 5	77
Chapter 6	86
Chapter 7	95
Chapter 8	106
Chapter 9	110
Chapter 10	115
Chapter 11	139
Chapter 12	149
Chapter 13	156
Chapter 14	171
Chapter 15	184
Also by RR Haywood	193

Season Five: The Rain

RYE

"We think. We plan. We Succeed.
And then Howie can kick the shit out of everything in his path."
-*Major Dillington-Campbell*

PROLOGUE

Friday
Mid-December
Six months before the outbreak…

'Oh my god, that hurts so much!' Howie said with a yelp as Bert, the security guard, leant in through the door to see Howie clutching his hand. 'Paper cut,' Howie said as though his arm was just severed at the shoulder.

Bert sucked air through his teeth with a grimace, 'Nasty. Sounds worse than that time I was shot through the leg.'

'Piss off. You were never shot through the leg.'

'I bloody was,' Bert said, propping his foot on a chair and yanking his sharply creased trouser leg up over his bulled boots. 'Right there.'

'Where?'

'There!'

'What's that?' Howie asked, peering at a faint red mark. 'What was it, an airgun?'

'You, cheeky sod,' Bert said as Howie grinned in that way he does. Charming, endearing, and with an ever-present air of self-effacing humour.

'Is that an actual bullet wound though?' Howie asked, dropping his tone to one of genuine interest.

'Aye. 7.62 round skimmed my calf in the Falklands.'

'I bet that bloody hurt.'

'Funnily enough, at the time, it didn't. Adrenalin pumping, and shells landing, and lads putting grenades in, and the jet fighters overhead. They were close, too. The Argies, I mean. They were coming at us, and we were going into them...' he trailed off. Lost in the memory of it as Howie stayed silent. 'Ach. Long time ago, mind, and yes, it bloody did hurt later when the shock wore off. But, and I'm not ribbing you, give me a 7.62 skim over a papercut any day. Right! I'd better to get to my station, Mr Howie, Sah!' he snapped a salute out and marched out of the office, leaving Howie wondering what it must be like to be in war and see, and do such things.

Howie knew he'd never be able to cope with it. Soldiers were something else. Heroic and brave, and full of courage, and they were fit and strong. He looked down at his slightly paunchy belly, then at the tiny papercut, still stinging like a bastard. A sudden feeling of emptiness, and a surge of worry that this was all he would ever know.

Is this it?

Is this all there ever will be?

But was that a bad thing?

Would he want bullets and bombs, and carnage, and war?

And if not, then what does he want?

Howie didn't know. Only that that feeling kept coming back.

But he didn't like that notion. It made him feel egotistical and entitled. That he alone of all the however many billions of people on this planet should *be* more or *have* more. And surely, if he was that driven, he would find a way to lead a more exciting life. Except, he never did anything to change it. He watched telly and ate the same food, and went to work, and went home, and watched telly.

He headed out of the duty manager's office to see Jermaine hadn't clocked in for his shift.

'Forgot to tell you. He's sick,' Michelle, the day turn manager, called as she walked out the door.

'Did you not call anyone in?' Howie called after her. 'Michelle?'

'What?'

'Did you not cover him?'

'Who?'

'Jermaine. You said he phoned in sick.'

'Yeah. He did.'

'Did you call anyone else in?'

'That's not my job,' she said dully with a shrug and walked off.

'That is exactly your job,' Howie said under his breath and went back in to see Dave walking by. 'Dave! Jermaine has gone sick. Can you help me do the fruit and veg; then I'll jump in with you on tinned goods. Is that okay?'

'Yes, Mr Howie,' Dave said because working in Tesco was sometimes a little bit like being in the military, with the same air of general chaos. Apart from not being allowed to kill people in Tesco.

They set to it and dragged the heavy cages filled with fresh produce into the fruit and veg section. Christmas music playing on a loop, and festive posters in every aisle, trying to pry the last few pennies from the hands of people, guilt-tripped into buying things they don't need.

A few late-night shoppers browsing slowly. The rain coming down outside. Lashing the big front windows and drumming noisily on the vast flat roof. It brought forth an altogether different feeling inside of Howie. For a second, he imagined he was somewhere tropical. Listening to the rain and hunkering down from a mission, or doing something cool. A sense of romance about the images in his head. A longing even. A need to change his life from what it was.

That happened sometimes. An active imagination coupled, he guessed, with a growing realisation that life wasn't fulfilling.

'You were in the army, Dave. Did you ever go to places with lots of rain?' Howie asked as they came to a stop.

'Yes.'

'Awesome. Great chat,' Howie said with a smile. Dave didn't smile. Not on the outside anyway. 'Where did you go?'

Dave hesitated because the question was too broad, and for a moment, he thought Mr Howie was asking him which locations Dave served in. Which Dave was not allowed to talk about. 'I can't say, Mr Howie.'

'Ooh. Gotcha. Right,' Howie said with an impressed look and a sudden urge to ask many more questions.

'I'll bring the other cages out, Mr Howie,' Dave said and walked off, leaving Howie standing still and trying to drown out the shit Christmas music and focus on the rain. Imagining himself somewhere awesome, hunkered down with his squad and listening to the rain while tending their injuries, like the gunshots they got from the war they're in. Like what Bert got, and by then, Howie would be all brave and brooding with an insanely hot girlfriend because it would be a different kind of war where girlfriends were allowed. At which point, Howie internally chastised himself for degrading his fictional love interest as merely being *the girlfriend*. Whereas, in fact, she could be another soldier, or a spy. Oh, that was sexy. Yeah, she'd be a spy, helping his team, and they'd all be like totally great guys that enjoyed hanging out. Which, sadly, was not something Howie had then.

'Ah, and there is the king within his kingdom,' a voice from behind. One that Howie recognised within a split second of hearing the first utterance, and he turned quickly, feeling surprised and also worried because his dad never came to see him at work.

'Dad?' Howie asked, looking up at his father. A tall man of otherwise average build. Dark hair turning grey, and a face that rarely showed emotions. 'What you doing here? Is mum okay?'

'Of course,' Howard said as though the question was not necessary. He offered a smile that didn't quite reach his eyes and glanced around. 'Thought you'd have people doing this for you, Howie.'

'Er, yeah, but not like *for* me. I mean, they work for Tesco. Not me, but Jermaine went sick, so I'm doing fruit and veg with Dave.'

'Dave? Is he here?'

'You know Dave?'

A second's worth of hesitation. 'You mentioned him!'

'I mentioned Dave? When?'

'I don't know, Howie. Probably at the last Sunday dinner. You said about a guy you worked with who is autistic.'

Howie shrugged. Figuring he must have said that for his father to know that about Dave. 'Yeah, he's pulling the cages out,' Howie said, turning to look around as Howard drew a small glass bottle from his coat pocket and pressed the plunger on the top, spraying a fine mist in the air between them. 'I said we'd do here; then I'd jump in with him on tinned goods... What's that smell?' Howie asks, turning back to see his father startling and looking nervous.

'What smell?'

'Like... Like antiseptic or something. Like a hospital smell,' Howie said, sniffing the air over the boxes of apples on the produce cages next to them.

'No idea. Right. Anyway. So, er, great.'

'Eh? You going already?' Howie asked as Howard turned away as though to leave.

'Well. Yes,' Howard said, blinking awkwardly. 'I was working late and, you know, just saying hello. So, hello... And goodbye.'

'Jesus, Dad,' Howie said as Howard glanced past Howie to keep an eye out for Dave.

'What?' Howard asked.

'Nothing,' Howie said with a slight sag and another shrug. 'Nice to see you. Say hi to mum.'

'Right. Yes. Bye then, Howie.'

'Bye,' Howie said, watching his father walk away. *'And great to see you, Dad. Oh, you too, Son. So great to see you. Here's a big hug, and wow, this is where you work, is it? And you're like the night manager? Did you want to see my office, Dad? I'd love to see your office, Son! Because I have literally never shown any interest in anything you do and just stopped by late at night on a Friday for no bloody reason other than to be really, really, really bloody awkward.* I mean. Fucking, really? Wait till I tell Sarah this one. *Hey, guess what our dad did?'* Howie muttered away to himself as he turned to lift the top crate of apples from the cage to see

Dave staring impassively. 'Okay. And now, this isn't awkward either...' Howie added. To which Dave said nothing. 'My dad was here.'

Dave didn't say anything about that either. Because Howard told Dave he should never talk about anyone from the team. Ever.

'But seriously though, can you smell antiseptic?' Howie asked as Dave nodded and thought that yes, he could, indeed, smell antiseptic.

'I'm not going mad then. Someone must have come out of hospital or something,' Howie said and stacked the box of organic Gala apples in the empty space on the shelf.

'I can refill if you are busy, Mr Howie,' Dave said, grabbing the next box to lift out of the cage.

'It's fine, mate. I quite like it if I'm honest. You okay though?'

'Yes, Mr Howie.'

'Do anything nice today?'

Dave didn't know what he could have done that would have been nice. He didn't do anything nice now at all. He worked at Tesco, then went home, and exercised, and stared at the walls. Then he slept and woke, and ate, and went back to work. He didn't do missions anymore. He didn't spend time with Carmen and Frank or go into the offices in London. He didn't travel to military bases around the world or do anything even similar to what he used to do. So, no. He didn't do anything nice. He never does anything nice. Except, Dave couldn't voice that because the emotions he felt would never form into words to give a reply. So he reverted to type and simply said, 'No, Mr Howie.'

'Excuse me. Can I get to the apples,' a very deep voice said as Howie blinked at the man mountain looming over him and stepped back to allow the guy to reach past and grab several Gala apples in one of his enormous hands. 'Thank you,' the guy said politely and headed off. Dressed in black like a bouncer and, no doubt, on his way to work in one of the nightclubs. A bald head, and the biggest shoulders Howie had ever seen, but he looked sad though. Lost even.

'Grab a bag, mate,' Howie called as the big guy turned back with a quizzical look. 'You've got five there. Bag of six is cheaper,' Howie said, taking one of the multi-bags from the cage to hand over as the big guy blinked down at him with sudden surprise at the act of kindness and said thank you before heading off. 'That's got to be a shit job,' Howie told Dave who stared blankly at him. 'Working the doors in a nightclub. It's bad enough here on the night shift. Pissheads and morons all bloody night. Anyway. Anyway. Let's get this done, then we can brew up. Eh. Dave? Nice cuppa?'

'Are they cheaper?' a woman asked. Blond hair. Blue eyes. Stunning. A younger woman with her. The same hair and eyes. The same coldness about them both. Mother and daughter out late, grabbing a few bits.

'The bags of apples, yes,' Howie said and handed one over.

'I don't like it though. I don't need therapy,' the daughter said as they walked off.

'Seriously though. I can still smell antiseptic,' Howie said to Dave.

They worked together for the rest of the night. Side by side, and even though Howie as the manager could have ordered someone else to do it, he didn't.

When the shift ended, Howie bid the others goodnight and walked out with Dave into the cold, windy winter pre-dawn darkness.

'See you tonight then, Dave.'

'Yes, Mr Howie.'

Howie headed home to his empty flat.

Dave does the same; except, his flat wasn't empty.

'Hello, Dave. Just checking in,' Howard said when Dave walked in to see Howard standing in the small living room of his one-bedroom flat. Dave didn't like it when Howard let himself in, but he stayed silent, without a flicker of reaction. 'All well?' Howard asked.

Dave nodded. There was a smell of antiseptic in the air. Mr Howie said he could smell it earlier, and Mr Howie also said his father had been to visit. Dave thought the smell was coming from Howard. He didn't ask though.

'Good. Great stuff. Right. Well. Monthly check all done then,' Howard said. 'Going forward, Dave, I think bi-monthly will suffice. Sorry. That means every other month.'

Dave knew what bi-monthly meant. He was autistic. Not stupid.

'Because you've obviously adapted very well to civilian life,' Howard added.

'Frank said ex-soldiers can find work as mercenaries.'

'When did you see Frank?' Howard asked sharply. 'Has he been here? Did Frank come here?'

'No, Mr Howard. Frank said this two years ago in Kabul.'

'Oh right! Like a chit chat thing? Right. Got it. And er, well, yes, some can, but sadly, not if they're autistic like you. So you need to stay here, Dave. Stay at Tesco, and er, like I said, just make sure Howie is alright.'

'Is this a mission?'

'No! Not at all. You're retired, Dave. But let's just say,' Howard said as he moved closer and lowered his voice. 'Between me and you, you do need to stay here, *on post, as it were.* Enough said? Yes?' Howard asked with a knowing wink that Dave had no clue about. 'Wonderful! Right. I'll see myself out. Good to see you, Dave.'

Howard left, and Dave ate cereal and went to bed, and even though his autism prevented him from voicing his emotions, he still felt that same thing that Howie felt.

That this was it, and this was all there ever would be.

Clarence worked in Boroughfare that night. His company had sent him down to cover the local football club's Christmas function. Which always kicked off and became a mini warzone of screaming women and angry thugs.

It was awful work. But what else could he do? He'd had enough of the private mercenary work and being in warzones, fighting conflicts that had nothing to do with him.

He stood in the corner of the large clubroom listening to the heated voices of drunk players and fans and the shrill tones of triggered women, and for a second, he thought about the dark-haired guy in the supermarket and how nice it was of him to say that about the apples.

Clarence was feeling invisible at that point. Like he'd ceased to exist in any meaningful form, and so, someone else looking past his size to see what he was buying and then offering help, as tiny a gesture as it was, really meant something.

Clarence also thought about the coach that pulled up in the Tesco car park as he left and the young women in sports gear that piled off while laughing.

It made him feel happy to see fit and healthy young people embracing life. Even the ginger stocky one that grinned at him as they passed.

'You're huge! Put a dress on and play hockey with us!' she said, but it was nice and cheerful, and Clarence didn't mind. She had a black eye. Clarence nodded at it. 'Should have seen the other girl,' Blinky joked and laughed as an attractive mixed-race woman bumped her from behind.

'Come along, Blinky.'

'Coming, Charles!'

Clarence ate some of the apples on the way to the function hall. He should have washed them first. Especially when he bit into the first one and thought it smelled of antiseptic; except, it didn't. The smell was on his hands, which came from the bag *containing* the apples. But then, he figured he'd eaten far worse in hellholes all over the world.

That night passed as they all do, with ejections from the club and constant scraps, and threats, and being groped by drunk women while beta males with gelled hair tried to belittle him.

He drove back to London and went home to his empty one room apartment, and ate cereals, and stared at the walls.

He felt low inside. Lost. Alone. Isolated. Cut off and filled with such sadness, it made a tear fall from his eye.

He brushed it away and told himself to buck up and embrace life, and seek happiness. Except, there was no happiness now. Just this feeling of emptiness while he faced a bleak and lonely future.

He even thought about suicide. Plenty of ex-military went out that way. Under their own steam from their own hands or means. Maybe that was his future. Maybe it would get so bloody awful, he'd end it himself.

He went to bed and felt like weeping.

Lilly rarely felt like weeping. She just wasn't a crier. Her mother was the same.

'How does that make you feel?' the therapist asked that Friday night in mid-December. A cosy office in a private clinic in Boroughfare that someone had recommended to Lilly's father.

'Why do I need therapy?' Lilly asked her father and mother when they'd booked it. 'I'm not mentally sick.'

'No. Of course not, Lilly,' her father said. A handsome but timid man with an ever-present air of fragility. 'But your mother and I...'

'We don't want you to become like me,' her mother said bluntly. Which was often her way.

Lilly didn't need to ask what that meant. Lilly was smart. Very smart, and she knew her father often struggled with his wife's emotionless manner and her lack of reactions. Lilly didn't think anything was wrong with it though.

'I can just, you know,' her father said and flapped his hands while looking wretched. 'No. Okay. Time for honesty, but this is said with love, Lilly. I love you deeply, and I care for you. I want you to know that.'

Lilly did know that. Her father said it all the time.

'But sometimes. Only sometimes. But now and then, you know, I can see, shall we say, *traits* of your mother in your behaviour and manner.'

'Which is because I have half of my genetic coding from my mother,' Lilly said.

'Which is super! So super. And great! And I love that, and I love you both so much, and Billy! I love Billy too.'

'Yes, Dad. We know you love us, but I don't need therapy,' Lilly said and turned away because that was that.

'Lilly. You have to do it,' Lilly's mother said.

'Why?'

'Because learning empathy and not being a cold-hearted bitch will help you *not* become a loser like me, working as a carer, wiping old people's arses.'

'No. No, that's not fair,' her father said with an intake of breath while looking crestfallen because he'd been wealthy when he'd met Lilly's mother, with a thriving business, but he was too nice. People took advantage, and he lost everything, which meant Lilly's mother having to pick shifts up as a carer.

'How will it help?' Lilly asked her mother bluntly, ignoring her father's eyes filling with tears.

Her mother shrugged. 'I will help you get a rich man.'

'I don't want a rich man.'

'There is more to life than money,' her father said.

'There isn't,' Lilly's mother told Lilly. 'Fine then. It will help you get money, however you get it.'

'Okay. That's not. That is not the reason,' her father said.

'It's stupid,' Lilly said. Because it was stupid. And she said that to the therapist. 'I think it's stupid.'

'Stupid that your mother and father care enough to try and help you? Or stupid for some other reason?' the therapist asked with a patronising smile.

'It's stupid that I need to pretend I care to satisfy the needs of insecure people. Likewise, therefore, I think coming here to be trained like a seal to smile and say things like *oh my gosh, that's so interesting! Tell me more,* or *oh no! I am so sorry that happened!*' Lilly said with mock sincerity. 'Is also stupid,' she added bluntly. 'And I know when to be nice and smile, unlike my mother. Who is like it all the time and probably has some kind of condition. I think my father actually likes it. She's very attractive and cold, but he's a wimp, so I think there's some strange fetish thing going on. Which is literally disgusting.'

'You think your father is a wimp? Why?'

'Because he is.'

'Do you love your father?'

'Yes. But do I respect him? No.'

'Do you respect your mother?'

Lilly thought about that for a moment. 'I respect her honesty, but I don't like the things she says to my dad, but then I don't like it that my dad doesn't stand up to her. But the point is, I am capable of showing warmth and care, and I am capable of laughing. The difference is that I will do it when I *need* to or when I *want* to. Not to please every other stupid person. Can I go now? Mum said we could pop into Tesco for groceries which, by any stretch of the imagination, is a far more positive experience than being here. But don't worry, I'll tell my dad it was *great and super, and just what we all needed!*'

Lilly finished with a big, warm smile that lit her face up, and which also made the therapist think that it was actually quite rare to meet a true sociopath. Lilly was right in what she said though. She did have emotions, and she had awareness, but she chose what to show and when.

Which would make Lilly's life ahead very interesting, especially, given that Lilly had inherited her father's very obvious intelligence and her mother's exceptional looks.

Lilly left therapy and got into the car with her mother. They didn't speak. But that wasn't abnormal.

'Was it good?' her mother asked when they pulled into the car park at Tesco.

'No,' Lilly said.

They walked in behind a massive guy with a bald head which made Lilly frown and look at her mother. That her mother was beautiful was obvious. Her father was a good-looking guy too, but he wasn't manly or masculine. Why didn't her mother go for someone like that massive man instead? 'Why did you marry dad?' she asked.

Her mother grabbed a basket and looked at her daughter for a second. 'You saw that big man and wondered why I didn't choose someone like that? I did. But he treated me badly. I got with your dad thinking I needed someone completely opposite, and your dad was charming and funny, and wealthy,' she paused with a bitterness flashing in her eyes. 'Then nine months later, you popped out.'

Something about the way she said that.

Something, something.

'Do you love him?' Lilly asked.

'I love my family in my own way' her mother said and walked off.

Lilly shrugged and followed her.

They got a few bits.

They got some apples.

They ate the apples in the car on the way home.

'Do they smell like soap?' Lilly asked as she bit into hers.

'After wiping arses all day, everything smells like soap,' her mother said. 'I hate my job, Lilly. I fucking hate it. Don't be poor, Lilly. Don't settle. Don't be timid. Don't ever be timid. Do what it takes to win. Don't be like me. I might not show emotion, but on the inside, I feel like fucking weeping every day.'

Charlie felt that way too sometimes. She came from wealth and had everything she could ever want, and she was the captain of the Under 21's England hockey team. Which meant, to her, that she had no right to feel that way.

She didn't feel it all the time. When she was with Blinky and some of the other girls, it was alright. They had a common purpose, and the comradery was always uplifting.

Like that night, after the local league game in Boroughfare. They'd won, as they often did, and after a couple of drinks with the other team, during which Blinky was forced to apologise to the players she punched and kicked and that one she headbutted, they got on the coach, with a pit-stop at the local Tesco for munchies.

Which is when the saw the goliath man walking out with a bag of apples.

'He looks sad,' Charlie remarked as they jostled their way across the car park. Blinky saw what she meant. The guy was huge, but he looked so down and beat, which is why Blinky veered over to grin and make a joke.

It seemed to brighten the guy's eyes for a second. Charlie gave him a nice smile too. He smiled back, and she saw the kindness in his eyes and wondered if his life was spent with people only ever seeing his size and not the man he was.

But life is fluid and forever moving, and so he walked away while they went inside the shop, with Charlie and Blinky grabbing apples and grapes.

'The bags of six are cheaper,' a dark-haired manager told them as he worked alongside a smaller man with a shaved head.

'Thank you, that's very kind,' Charlie said in her educated voice.

'S'fine, mate. She's loaded,' Blinky said with a nod at Charlie. The dark-haired guy smiled and went about his work. The shaven-haired smaller man didn't show any reaction at all.

They got back on the coach and headed home, with Charlie eating an apple that tasted a bit weird. 'What is that?' she asked and held it near Blinky's nose. Blinky pretended to lean closer but bit into it, and pulled it out of Charlie's hand. 'That was mine, you greedy wotsit. There's a whole bag there.'

'I wanted your gob inside of me,' Blinky said with a mock sexy wink and a mouthful of apple as Charlie snorted a laugh. 'And that's like disinfectant or something. It's wot us poor people use to clean things in our workhouses.'

'Very funny,' Charlie said as Blinky took another bite. 'Well, don't eat it then!'

'S'fine. They wouldn't use dangerous cleaners around food. So, what you doing this weekend?'

Charlie sagged with a heavy sigh. 'My parents' are back.'

Charlie's father had been away on a business trip, and her mother had been on a spa break with a friend, but Charlie knew her mother had been away with a lover. Her father had lovers too. She even figured they both knew about each other's lovers, but for some reason, they stayed together.

As Charlie got older, she realised that was only because of their combined wealth and reputation, and power, and nothing to do with love.

That made her incredibly sad, but worse, she felt resentment towards them for the constant pressure they applied to shape her life like theirs. Its like she was living it for them, and that it wasn't her own.

'Let's talk about your future.'

That was the line her father always used, often within

seconds of seeing her again. Even if he'd been away for weeks.

'You're nearly twenty-one, Charlotte. We need to think about the potential partnerships for your future betrothal.'

She hated the way he said it. The formality of it, and the way it was like another deal to be made.

'What about Angus? His father is the majority stakeholder in-.'

'God, no. He's a horrible man,' Charlie said.

'Who? Angus, or the father?'

'Both!'

'That other one then. The Jew. What's his name? Is the Jew boy called David?' her father asked her mother.

'Yes,' she said without looking up from her phone.

'Must you call him the Jew?' Charlotte asked.

'But he is a Jew.'

'And all those talks you give against racism?' she asked.

'What of them? I'm black. Not Jewish. But David's family are worth billions.'

'David is gay.'

'He's having a phase,' her father said as though the young man was simply into heavy metal or something. 'Ah. Sayeed asked after you. Well. He asked his father who asked me in Dubai. I said you were keen to see him again.'

'Good match,' her mother said, looking up sharply. 'He's pretty much a Saudi prince.'

'I would like to find my own partner.'

'Good god, not this again,' her mother said and slammed the phone down. 'We have been through this, Charlotte. You know you don't make wise decisions.'

'You don't make wise decisions,' her father said.

'We gave you freedom, and look what you did. You used it to play hockey with that awful *girl* with the ginger hair.'

'Hockey,' her father said while giving her a glare.

'You have to think of the family name, Charlotte. Doyle-Finnerly has a reputation,' her mother said.

'We have a reputation,' her father added. 'Look at your mother and I. Our parents chose wisely, and we've enjoyed a very good return of investment and highly lucrative terms based on our coupling.'

'What about love? What about *being in love?*'

'We have discussed this, Charlotte!' her mother snapped as though exasperated. 'Emotions do not mix in business.'

'A marriage isn't business.'

'A marriage is the single biggest business venture one can make!' her father said. 'Enough of this. You will show cooperation and court with who we see fit that matches with your station and intelligence.'

Charlie had that argument many times. But it never did any good. Her mother and father were highly skilled negotiators and always flipped the script in ways that made Charlie feel manipulated.

She felt pressured too. She shouldn't, but she did, and that brought on a sense of despondency that her university and hockey days were drawing to an end, and she'd either do as her family ordered or be ostracised.

It made her feel empty and worthless. That she was a *thing* and not a person, and that everyone else had the right to make decisions for her, rather than being allowed to respond to her own emotional states as anyone else would.

She slipped into silent thought that night as the coach made its way home. Blinky did the same. Sitting beside her and thinking ahead to lonely days in her bedsit that would be spent longing to be back on the pitch, training. A broken home. A broken life. Too aggressive. Too angry. Too direct and outspoken. Charlie was the only one that *got her*. Blinky's future was bleak too. Find a shitty job doing something shitty and grow old, and die.

'I need a piss,' Blinky said. 'Has this coach got a bog?'

'I don't think so,' Charlie said.

'Oi, driver! I need a piss,' Blinky called to the front.

'Wait till we get back!'

'Who the fuck is he talking to? Who the fuck are you talking to? I'll piss on your fucking seats, mate!'

'Jesus, Blinky,' Charlie said, trying to pull her friend back. 'Just pull over and let her go.'

'Where?' the driver shouted while gesturing around at the urban sprawl.

'I don't give a shit. I'll do it here,' Blinky said and started tugging her joggers down.

'Alright! Fuck me,' the driver said as he pulled the coach over.

'How hard was that, bellend?' Blinky asked as she dropped out and headed behind a small bush to piddle at the edge of a car park as Charlie noticed a woman outside a small block of offices smoking a cigarette.

'Sorry! She needed to go,' Charlie called.

'It's okay!' Paula called back with a wave of her hand.

'My piss is organic though, so it's like totally fine,' Blinky said as Paula smiled and puffed on her cigarette, and looked at the ginger girl with a black eye and the attractive mixed-race woman. Both in sports clothing and obviously coming back from a match. It made Paula feel both happy and sad at the same time. Happy for them to be enjoying themselves, but sad at her own life. It made her wish she had the freedom to go and play team sports, and do fun things.

They got back on the coach, but the ginger one came

back out after swearing profusely at the driver. 'Here!' she yelled and lobbed an apple over to Paula who caught it one-handed. 'Fuck! Good catch! You're wasted working there!'

Paula laughed and waved them goodbye, and headed back inside to stare at spreadsheets, so she could help absurdly rich people pay less tax.

She was in her thirties and felt like had nothing to show for it. She had a good income, but for what? She didn't have time to do anything with it.

It made her feel weird inside. Like it was all wrong and empty, and meaningless, and she longed for something else, but she didn't know what that was.

She shrugged it off as she always did and figured everyone gets like that.

But it was getting harder. She felt lost and alone, and that it was all so meaningless, and those same thoughts kept coming back into her mind.

Was this it?

Was this all there ever would be?

She pushed the thoughts away and bit into an apple, and for a moment, she thought she could smell antiseptic, but put it down to the soap she used after washing her hands. She glanced out the window to the traffic lights, and a van pulled up with a good-looking guy at the wheel, but he looked anxious, terrified even. Paula wondered what had made him that way, but the lights changed, and the van went, on and Roy soon caught up with the coach ahead, carrying Charlie and Blinky.

That annoyed Roy because it was going too slowly, and he had to get to hospital before he died of cancer. The cyst on his back. The tiny one that had been checked by many doctors who all told him it was not now and never would be cancerous. That cyst hurt a tiny bit earlier when he did some floor exercises, which obviously meant it had turned evil and was spreading cancer through his body faster than any chemo or radiotherapy could stop.

He tried to distract himself. He even went into a supermarket in Boroughfare and bought apples and magazines, and other random things he paid no attention to. It smelled a bit of antiseptic in the fruit and veg section, which made Roy worry that someone else had a disease or something, so he rushed out.

Not that it mattered because he was dying anyway.

Those thoughts filled his life and mind, and every waking moment of his existence.

They made him become isolated from society, which, in turn, increased the paranoia, and so his life was spent in misery, with his mind forever thinking *Is this it? Is this all I ever will be?*

The next town along, Roy pulled in to the car park of the regional hospital and jumped out so fast that the bag of apples he bought from Tesco in Boroughfare fell from the van.

A moment later, he was inside the emergency room, begging to be seen as a tall, handsome, young man walked glumly through the car park and stopped on seeing the bag of apples.

Nick was hungry.

Nick was always hungry.

But he was also always broke. He looked around but couldn't see the owner of the apples. They were close to a van, and from the positioning, he figured they must have fallen when the driver got out.

Nick's mind was good like that. He could see things that were obvious to him that other people found very confusing. Like wiring circuits or engines, or schematics, and drawings, and how things worked. Which was a great skill, unless you didn't know how to read. Because not being able to read meant he could never get work and use those skills, or undertake further education.

And so, he spent days walking and doing nothing. Like right then, when he saw the bag of apples and picked them up, and put on the van bonnet. Then, he paused and apologised to anyone listening, and took just one of the Gala apples to eat.

He hoped the owner wouldn't mind, and he also hoped that whatever the owner was at the hospital for was nothing serious.

He walked on and ate the apple which tasted a bit odd, and he looked at signs he couldn't read in a world that he felt no connection to. Alone. Lost. Isolated.

He felt empty inside. Tall. Handsome. Young. Fit. But sad. So very sad, and he wondered, as he walked nowhere in particular and ate the apple, if this was all there ever would be in his life.

※ ※

An hour later, Roy walked out of the hospital, having been told, yet again, that it was just a harmless fatty lump.

He headed to the next town over, and such was his mental state and distraction that he paid no attention to the bag of five remaining apples caught in the dip where the bonnet meets the windscreen.

Not even when he pulled up at traffic lights, and a young man with blond hair and blue eyes walking by spotted them and tried to call out, but Roy was listening to folk music and didn't hear. He turned the corner, and the bag of apples slid off the bonnet and into the hands of the young man with blue eyes who darted out to catch them.

'And now, I've got five apples,' Cookey said as he watched the van drive off. 'Which is perhaps the most interesting thing that has happened the whole of this year,' he told himself as he fished an apple out and bit into it. He paused and thought he should wash them first, especially seeing as they smelled a bit like antiseptic or something, but his mum always said only wimps and pansies washed fruit and veg, and so he ate it anyway. Mind you, his mother was nearly always drunk and angry, or passed out. And it's not like there was ever any fresh fruit and veg anyway. Unless she was sober enough to go to the foodbank.

But anyway. It didn't matter because Cookey now had five apples which brightened his day no end, being a young man with a mostly positive outlook on life, and so he bounced along aimlessly, eating an apple and smiling at the people passing him by, which is what he did most of the time because there wasn't anything else to do.

Which is why he kept thinking about joining the army. Cookey didn't see himself as a soldier, but anything had to be better than this. He was feeling it more and more lately that his life was empty and dull. He needed to be around people he could make laugh.

'Alright darlin!' a jeering voice across the street. Three lads heckling a young woman covered in tattoos walking past them. She flicked them a middle finger and walked on. 'Yeah, you fucking want some!' one of the lads shouted and rubbed his own groin as he went after her with his mates. The three of them drunk and loud, and dangerous.

'Fuck off,' the woman said with an eyeroll like she wasn't bothered, but Cookey could see her nerves.

'We'll fuck something alright,' the lad said in a tone that

made the glint of humour in Cookey's eye fade away. It was late and dark, and the woman was alone. He swallowed and readied to call out.

'Shut your fucking mouth and leave her alone,' a hard voice snapped, followed by a young man with an equally hard face coming around the corner to walk past the woman towards the three lads.

Cookey stopped and stared with the half-eaten apple in his hand, and wished he was brave like that, but the lad was also bloody stupid because he was on his own, and the other three were bigger than he was.

'Who the fuck are you, cunt?' one of the drunk men snarled, and it turned ugly fast, and he charged at the lad. But the lad stayed put right until the last second, then his hand whipped out with a brutal hook that sent the obnoxious drunk flying off his feet.

'Fuck!' Cookey said and started running because the other two went for the guy at the same time. 'Get off him!' Cookey yelled and punched one away, and the three drunks grabbed one another and ran off shouting abuse from a safe distance.

'Thank you!' the tattooed woman called.

'S'alright,' the hard-faced lad said.

'Want an apple?' Cookey called to her. She grinned and said okay. He threw one over.

'Cheers!' she said and went off.

'Do you want an apple?' Cookey asked the other lad.

'Are they washed?'

'No.'

The other lad shrugged and took one to bite into. 'Cheers. Why do they smell of antiseptic?'

'Yeah, I thought that,' Cookey said as they shrugged and

ate them anyway. 'So, like, was that like Karate or something?'

'Karate is for middle aged accountants. I used to box.'

'Why don't you still box now?'

Blowers shrugged and bit into the apple. He stopped boxing when he got kicked out of the Marines. He stopped everything when he got kicked out of the Marines because it wasn't fair, and it wasn't right. He'd spent years training for it and was the highest performing recruit in his intake. He excelled at everything during his Commando training.

Then, at the very end, some fucking twat delivering food to the base almost ran him over. Blowers had to leap out the way. The truck clipped his ankle and caused a stress fracture, and that was it. He was out.

He said he was fine.

He said he could strap it up and keep going.

They said no.

They said to let it heal and re-apply in another year.

That nearly broke Blowers because it meant going home to his shitty bedsit. No hope. No future. No family. His father left years ago. His mother moved away with a guy. They were never close anyway.

He spent hours walking and doing nothing. He felt lost and alone. The same as they all did. That same feeling.

'You should join the army or something, with skills like that,' Cookey said as Blowers gave him a glare but saw kindness and compassion staring back at him.

'Yeah. Maybe. Cheers for helping though.'

'Yeah, it was the half an apple I threw that made them run off.'

Blowers snorted a laugh at the way the other lad said that, and he hadn't smiled in a very long time.

Cookey and Blowers became friends that night.

They became the best of friends, and although Cookey could have joined earlier, he waited for Blower's ankle to fully heal, and they signed up together.

❧ ❧

Tappy got heckled a lot. Tattoos and a curvy body, and a pretty face often attracted bad attention, but it was nice to know good men still existed, and the apple was a nice touch.

Even if it did taste a bit like soap. She ate it as she rushed on to work behind the bar in a nightclub. It wasn't her chosen job. She was a mechanic, and a very good one, but most garages didn't want to hire curvy, pretty, tattooed women, and those that did were not because of her skills with engines. She'd learned to spot a pervert a mile off.

She wanted to be back in her father's workshop, but there just wasn't enough work for her dad to pay her. Times were hard, and more cars were run by electronics which were fixed more by diagnostics and less by stripping them down the old-fashioned way.

So she pulled pints and worked casual jobs, and smiled, and joked her way along while inside she felt that ever increasing sense of angst. That this was all it would ever be. That life was passing by with no meaning or purpose.

She went out the back for some fresh air on her break later and leant against the wall. A scuffle at the end where the alley met the street. A stocky, black guy pushed another man against the wall.

'Pay up. Now!'

'Fuck's sake, alright,' the other guy said and pulled a roll of bank notes from his pocket that the black guy snatched away. 'Don't take it all!'

'You owe more than this.'

'I got kids!'

'Then don't do drugs.'

'Lads,' Tappy called as the black guy shot her a look. He was good looking and seemed smart, and nodded as though he understood, and simply walked off with the money.

'That was for my kids,' the other man said with a whine as he motioned to Tappy.

'Don't do drugs then,' she told him and went back inside as Maddox Doku tucked the cash into his pocket and got back in the car to head back to his estate.

'You get it, yeah?' Darius asked as Maddox got in the front passenger seat.

'Sweet, bro!' Mo Mo said with a grin in the back with Jagger.

They drove back to their estate. Back to their broken lives and broken homes, and feral existences. Mo's mother selling herself for booze and drugs. Maddox in and out of prison. No hope. No future. No sense of belonging. That same feeling inside of them that showed in their faces as they drove in silence.

Is this it?

Is this all it ever will be?

Their car stopped at traffic lights in the next town, and they all looked right to a young, black man with big, sad eyes, walking past, eating an apple that had a weird taste that his mum bought from the Tesco in Boroughfare.

The four lads in the car didn't see the bruises on his body or the belt-whip marks on his back from the constant beatings given to Danny by his stepfather.

That's why Danny spent hours out of the house, walking the streets and longing to be old enough to join the army and get away from here.

That same sense of despair inside of him.

THE UNDEAD TWENTY-SIX   29

Isolation and hopelessness.

The same in all of them.

The car drove on, but the sight planted a seed and Maddox told Darius to head into Boroughfare.

'Why here?' Darius asked.

'They've got an all-night Tesco,' Maddox said, and they drove to the car park and went inside so Maddox could buy some apples as two of the staff spoke with a Tesco lorry driver near the fruit and veg section.

'I'm sorry, alright? The Isle of Wight don't have anything cos of a mix-up, so every store has to give up their extras.'

'But it's Saturday tomorrow,' the dark-haired manager said as he worked with a smaller guy with a shaved head to load boxes of fruits onto pallets. 'We'll be sold out by mid-morning. Then what? Are the Isle of Wight gonna send it back?'

'They're putting on extra deliveries,' the lorry driver said as Maddox took his apples to the self-service checkout and told Mo Mo and Jagger to put the stuff they'd nicked back on the shelf.

'We've got a car full of coke and money. We're not getting pinched so you can nick a bottle of JD.'

'And Haribo,' Mo Mo said with his cheeky grin, but they put it back as Bert chuckled to himself in the office with the phone in his hand ready to call the police.

Maddox headed off back to his estate, and the lorry driver worked with Howie and Dave to take produce from the Boroughfare store which was added to the stocks taken from other stores.

He then drove south to Portsmouth and got a late-night ferry to Fishbourne on the Isle of Wight, and drove the short distance into Ryde on the northern shore, to the big Tesco store that had ran out of all fruit and veg the day before due to a computer ordering error.

And because it was the island's biggest supermarket, the lack of stock made the local news, as did the sudden replenishment, which is what prompted Marcy to head up to her local Tesco after finishing work in the hotel in the early hours.

She stocked up on a few essentials and grabbed a bag of Gala apples. They were her brother's favourites.

'Apples, Marcy!' Davey said when she got home.

'Why are you still awake?' she asked him. But he always stayed up until she got home. He was autistic, and the adherence to routines were very important to his well-being. They ate an apple each, which Marcy realised smelled of soap or something, and she made him stop, so she could wash them, even though they'd already eaten half an apple each.

She wiped apple juice from her brother's chin and gave him her genuine smile as she handed the washed apple back. But she felt sad inside. That this was all life was, and that this was all she could ever do for her brother and mum. Working cash-in-hand and wearing low-cut tops to get tips from blokes, and taking the pats on her arse and the constant comments. Day after day. Week after week.

Was this it?

Was this all there ever would be?

Reginald felt that same thing. In his flat in Newport, the county town of the Isle of Wight. A gifted intellectual, but he was timid and nervous and preferred to stay home and read, and study. His home delivery came the following morning from Tesco. He packed it all away neatly and washed the apples thoroughly. But some chemicals are absorbed quickly, and so by the time the apples were washed, the thing that was on them was inside of him.

He ate one as he sat down at his desk.

Books open in front of him. Spread across his table. A very great mind held within his head. A mind that could process information far quicker than most, but it would never be tested. He'd never be able to do anything with it. He did a few pub quizzes, but the other teams started to hate the way he always won, and it was simply not challenging enough.

Reginald longed to be challenged properly. Except, he didn't know by what method or how that would ever happen, and as the years went by, he grew to accept that such a thing would never happen. There were no foes out there that had to be outwitted. Such things were fantastical and absurd, and so this really was it. This really was all there ever would be.

That same Saturday, and while Howie slept, Bashir called into the Tesco in Boroughfare to hand in his CV and covering letter to the customer service desk. He was desperate for employment and taking the bus to every big town in the south to ask for work.

Except, nobody wanted to hire an ex-soldier from Afghanistan who could only understand basic military instructions in English.

That same feeling inside. That this was it. That this was all there ever would be. He bought a single apple. It was all he could afford, and he sat outside in the sun and ate it.

He remembered sitting in the sun and eating rations with US Delta forces, and then later, with the British SAS when he undertook missions with them. Taking out the Taliban and trying to rid his country of the rot that infested it.

He fought hard and killed many, and he was promised, as they all were, along with the interpreters like his brother's wife, Damsa, that they would be looked after and given visas to either the US or the UK.

But that never happened.

The US and the UK pulled out of Afghanistan and never honoured their promises.

The Taliban took swift revenge and killed many.

Damsa's son had been notified that he would be given a scholarship for a music school because of his skills playing the violin. Ameer and his family would be given housing, but they had to pay and arrange their own travel into the UK.

The family started planning a way out of Afghanistan, but that took time, and the Taliban were closing in.

They came one night.

Eight men armed with Kalashnikovs.

Bashir heard them coming. He hid in the shadows and slit the first man's throat in silence. He took the headscarf and disguised himself, and got up close to the next two, and took them down.

One of them had a grenade. He went outside in the moonless night and put the grenade into the shed the others were hiding in. They tried to run, but Bashir gunned them all down.

They fled that night and over the next few weeks, Bashir begged, bribed, and murdered to keep them moving into Pakistan, then through Iran, and into Turkey, and through the Balkans, until they finally arrived at the migrant camps in Calais.

They thought that last leg would be easy. It was one short boat ride to the UK, but the traffickers wanted such high fees it was impossible.

They said Damsa could offset some of the cost off as a sex worker. She was attractive and would make get good money in Dubai.

They refused, and the situation grew desperate. They had no money or food. Their clothes were rags, and winter was coming.

The men came back again. Two of them. One was Eastern European. The other was African. They said the fees to get across the channel had gone up again, but they could still take Damsa. They said they could take her anyway because the French didn't give a shit about migrants. Nobody did. Hundreds drowned nearly every month, and nobody cared.

They said they'd come back the next day.

They said they would send Ameer the boy over the channel if Damsa went with them.

Bashir tracked the men as they left the camp.

He followed them to their car at an isolated spot along the coast in a thicket of bare trees.

He called out to them and put his hands together to show meekness and mercy. They said angry words, but his manner allowed him to get in close to draw the knife and stab the African in the throat. The European tried to pull a pistol, but Bashir pushed the African into him, then stabbed him in the back many times until he was dead.

He put their bodies in the car and set it on fire.

He stole all of their money and used it to pay another trafficker to get the family across the channel into the UK where the music school honoured their offer and housed Damsa, Maleek, and Ameer. The family used their benefits to help Bashir and his brother Tajj, and they were glad to be safe and away from death, and able to apply for refugee status, but the days turned into weeks and months, and that same feeling came back inside of Bashir.

Was this it now?

Was this all there ever would be?

He was a skilled soldier. He could be of service, but he sat and ate that apple – with a slight frown at the smell of antiseptic on his hands - and felt nothing but hopelessness.

Henry felt that sense of hopelessness too.

In the briefing room in their offices in Whitehall, London on the following Monday.

It showed on his face as Frank shrugged, and Carmen bit her bottom lip while George tutted in that calm, polite way of his.

'Nothing,' Henry said.

'Nope. Nothing,' Carmen said.

'He's had some help,' Henry said again. 'Someone like Neal Barrett doesn't just disappear.'

'He's a very intelligent man,' Carmen said. 'He's got a doctorate.'

'In statistics,' Henry said.

'I'm with her,' Frank said with a nod at Carmen as Howard bustled into the room. 'Here he is. What happened? Did you have to count the paperclips?' Frank asked.

'Wasn't funny twenty years ago, Frank,' Howard said as he slipped his jacket off and sat down at the conference table, and clocked the look coming from Henry who hated tardiness and poor time keeping. But Henry could fuck off. So could Frank. Howard was sick of them all. He was sick of the constant jibes from Frank about counting stationary and not being a field agent, and he was sick of being at their beck and call. The team had done good work over the years, but familiarity breeds contempt, and that contempt was barely concealed.

'Doctor Barrett?' Henry asked, holding that look on Howard.

'What of him, Henry?'

'It has been three months since the operation,' Henry said, meaning the secret massing of scientists in the mountain facility in Switzerland that Frank and Carmen had infiltrated and managed to cultivate Neal Barrett into being an asset. Except, by then, three months later, Neal had disappeared without trace, and all of the scientists that had been vocally in opposition to the release of the cull had been murdered before they could leak anything.

'That's a negative from me,' Howard said.

'What you saying it like that for?' Frank asked.

'Soldiers say negative.'

'Yea, but you're not a soldier. Whatever. Up to you if you want to sound like a cunt.'

'Alright,' Henry said before it could escalate.

George listened on with benign interest. Henry's right-hand man. Second in command of the team. A captain in the Parachute Regiment, then latterly in the SAS before he seconded into the British Security Services.

At any other time or in any other unit, George would have gained leadership a long time ago. He was an exceptional soldier. A brilliant leader. A gifted strategist and an outstanding agent.

But Henry was better.

Every security agency in the world knew of Major Henry Campbell-Dillington. He was feared and respected in equal measure from the CIA to MOSSAD, to terrorist cells all over the world.

And next to someone like Henry, George would always only ever be the second in command.

It grated on him.

It infuriated him.

He grew resentful, but he never showed it. Not once. Not a flicker.

Always be polite. That was George's mantra. Along with a few others that he used to destabilise regimes and military units, and political movements all over the world.

Carmen was feeling different things too. There was a disquiet inside. Something very big and very terrible was going to happen to the world if they didn't stop it. But then, there was always something big and terrible that was about to happen. Nuclear war. Anthrax. Mass uprisings. She'd seen enough of it. She was becoming restless, and more and more lately, she couldn't see the lines between good and bad. She couldn't tell if they were the good guys.

'Right. We clear all other tasks and focus on finding Neal,' Henry said, bringing them all back from their thoughts.

The meeting disbanded. Henry returned to his office with a growing feeling of failure inside. That he was powerless to stop this thing from happening. It ran deep. He knew that because all trace of that secret facility in Switzerland, and what happened inside of it, had disappeared.

Henry had made a verbal report to Alistair Appleton. The minister in charge of clandestine covert teams operating within the domestic and overseas security portfolio, of which there were a few. Alistair had listened intently and said he would deal with it.

Henry expected to be re-tasked very swiftly. To start assassinating or arranging the deaths of key players while George was deployed to infiltrate and destabilise any identified hierarchies.

Except that never happened.

A month or so after making that report, Henry arranged to be in a deserted corridor at the time of Alistair Appleton walking through. Alistair barely made eye-contact with Henry. And when he did, he made no sign of recognition and gave no greeting.

And it was that single act that made Henry realise this thing did, indeed, run very deep, which is why they needed to find Neal to get his testimony and protect him from the other security teams, and to recover the list of people with natural immunity.

But they had no leads. Even Howard wasn't generating anything.

There was another aspect to it that lit a slow burning fuse deep within Henry, because while it was clear that whatever was happening had deep connections within government, it was also clear he wasn't being invited in.

Which meant they either feared his honesty too much, or – and the idea that Henry hated most of all – they were disregarding his ability to stop it.

He rubbed his face, then pulled his hands away from the faint scent of antiseptic. Carmen smelled it too in the main room. 'Can you smell it?' she asked Frank.

'What? This?' Frank asked and lifted an arse cheek before farting.

'Twat. Antiseptic. Oh god. Frank! That's disgusting,' she said and retreated into the corridor between their offices, and again, caught the smell of antiseptic. It was coming from Howard's office. 'It's you!' she said.

'What is?' Howard asked bluntly.

'Antiseptic. It's coming from you,' she said and walked into his office, which Howard hated, and sniffed this way and that before making a beeline for his outer jacket.

'Really, Carmen?' Howard asked with an irritated tut. 'I have to make a call.'

'It's on your coat,' she told him.

'What is?'

'That smell of antiseptic. You must have got anti-bac gel on it or something.'

Howard knew it wasn't antiseptic or anti-bacterial gel either.

It was something else.

It was a vaccine.

Carmen left his office with a glance to Henry looking dark and frustrated at his desk. She shared a smile with George who was always polite, and she went back into the main office to the lingering stench of Frank's farts. Which used to be funny.

Now, they weren't.

That feeling inside of her.

Was this it?

Was this all there ever would be?

The same for all of them. That feeling of being lost and trapped in meaningless lives with no real connections. Full of anxieties and depressions. Full of fears. Isolated and lonely.

Bibi Thapa felt the same. The son of a renowned family

that had served the British Gurkha regiments with pride and gained many medals.

His future was destined to be the same, but he held a secret that burned his insides with shame, and though he laughed and joked with the other lads at Christ's Hospital School about which girl had the best legs or boobs, he simply didn't look at women that way.

Johnny became his best friend. Gifted at Judo. Strong as an ox. His father was the UK's foremost Judo instructor who coached Olympic athletes. He pushed Johnny relentlessly. Up before dawn seven days a week. Johnny won medals and excelled, but the pressure and constant pushing without love made him develop a stammer. His father hated that. He said it made Johnny sound weak, and he told him not to talk unless he could do it properly. That only made it worse, and so Johnny was glad he got a place at Christ's Hospital School.

Ali was too. Ali Chong. But that was never her name. Her name was Ali Yeong. The Chong family died in the same container that Ali Yeong was found inside of on the back of a lorry in an industrial estate near Dover when she was five years old.

Everyone else was dead. All forty of them. Ali's mum and her aunts, and Ali's sisters, and brother, and somehow, within all the confusion and chaos that followed, the police and social services said she must be Ali Chong.

She was orphaned and put through foster homes until, eventually, she ended up at the school where she met Tamara. Black British. Funny. Warm. Always smiling. Her father was stabbed to death in Croydon. He'd only just left the Navy. It devastated her mother. She became *too religious* and spent every waking hour at church. Some family friends stepped in. They knew Christ's Hospital had a strong connection to the military services and arranged a place for Tamara.

It became a refuge for her. As it did for Ali and Bibi, and Johnny. They became a unit that looked out for each other. They had each other's backs and went through military cadet training together. They shared their secrets. Their fears. Their worries.

At weekends, they went out together. They were older students. Seventeen. Eighteen. They had greater freedom, *and* they were part of the Christ's Hospital Regiment number one squad.

They went out that weekend too.

They went for a drive in Tamara's car.

They went to Boroughfare, to the all-night supermarket.

They saw a team of hockey players getting onto a coach.

They saw a huge man that looked sad.

They saw a mother and daughter with blond hair and blue eyes not talking to each other.

They saw a dark-haired manager working with a small man with a shaved head in the fruit and veg section.

Tamara bought grapes. Ali bought a net of satsumas. Johnny bought chocolate bars.

'F... F... Fuckmydad!' he blurted with a grin.

Bibi smiled at a guy walking by. The guy smiled back and paused as though to make chat. An air of understanding instantly between them. But Bibi turned away and bought a bag of apples.

They got back in Tamara's car and shared their food.

'What is that?' Tamara asked, sniffing her hands. 'Is that antiseptic?

And so, it spread.

One spray from one bottle.

But the mist it created touched many of the bags of apples, and in turn, that mist and the chemical within it, namely a tweaked version of the Panacea, touched many pairs of hands and was ingested into the central nervous systems of many different people.

Most of whom showed no reaction whatsoever.

But to a few.

A few people with certain genetic types.

It lay dormant.

Waiting.

Waiting to be activated when this world ended.

And the Brave New World began.

1

**Day Thirty
Sunday 14ᵗʰ August**

A NEW DAWN COMES IN THIS BRAVE NEW WORLD, BUT for the first time in weeks, it's not glorious sunshine heralding the start to another beautiful day, but it's grey and muted, and the sky is filled with full, dark clouds from which the rain pours down.

In the front passenger seat of the SUV, Henry grimaces at the water coming through the empty space where the windscreen was before they smashed it out from being cracked and full of spider-web fractures from the detonation of Gatwick.

Carmen and Bashir ride in the back while Frank drives. All of them filthy. All of them cut, wounded, and bruised. Their clothes soaked and torn. Singed and burnt in places. Bashir's legs exposed from his trousers catching alight when they hunkered down behind the utility building when the silos went up and turned day into night.

Gaffer tape around a wound on Frank's arm. A deep, ragged cut on Henry's bald head. Carmen's top torn from being bitten on the shoulder, with claw marks from talon-like fingernails from her neck to her cheek.

But it was the heat that really hurt.

That heat.

That was something else.

They still feel hot now. Like they've been baked in an oven and are still cooking on the inside.

It's no different in the armoured van ahead of them.

Roy driving. His back cut open from the incredible melee when they were all taken down. It's deep too, and he leans forward to stop his blood and rain-soaked shredded top from pressing against the seat.

Howie in the back, standing next to the broken sliding door that buckled from, first, being kicked by a furious Jess in full temper at being contained while Charlie was in trouble, and then, from the detonation of Gatwick.

An explosion that rocked the van and blew every window out from every building in a radius of hundreds of metres, and tore bricks from buildings and whole walls, and chimney stacks that slammed into the van with Reginald inside. Buckling the panels. Cracking the armoured glass. The blast was so powerful it made the van spin and slam into a wall, twisting the chassis.

It still drives, but Roy has to fight to keep it straight, and he can hear the axles grinding and can feel the vibrations through his feet. Especially when he touches the brakes.

The Saxon slows in front. Navigating a turn. The van does the same, and Howie hears and feels the vibrations and noises of metal on metal. Sparks at the back. He leans out to see another flurry of them. Bright and almost pretty in the rain. They should stop and find something else, but what? And where from?

They can hardly see more than a few metres in this rain, and the people inside the vehicles are just as fucked as the vehicles themselves. Howie's no different. His clothes torn, and his body a tapestry of fresh wounds, cuts, and bruises on top of all the others, built up from thirty days of fighting since the world as they knew it ceased to be.

He frowns with a thought as the rain soaks his face.

'How many?' he starts to ask as he looks to Reginald, but the words fail from his throat being thick and hoarse. He starts to clear his throat, but Reginald knew what he was going to ask.

'Thirty days today,' the small man replies.

Howie looks at him for a second, then stares back out into the rain, feeling like his insides are still baking.

That heat.

That was something else.

He could lie down in an ice-bath and still feel hot.

'Jesus, thirty days,' Paula murmurs. Her back to the side of the van. Both of her hands holding Clarence's in her lap, with his one hand bigger than both of hers.

He grunts and stirs. She smiles up at him and glances at the cauterised stump wrapped in gaffer tape where his right hand was.

'Does it hurt?'

'I'm alright,' he says quietly, deeply. The pain is immense. It didn't hurt so much when it happened because that was mid-battle, and even straight after when Dave cut the last tendon and Meredith snatched the hand up and ran off – even then the pain wasn't so bad, mind you, Paula was giving him a kiss at the time.

But now though.

Yeah. It hurts a lot.

But still.

That heat.

That was the real killer, and the sweat still beads on his bald head and pours down his cheeks, blackened from grime and soot.

Paula the same. Hot. Soaked through. Exhausted and desperately hungry. It's not over either. They have to get back to Camber and clean weapons, and make-ready, and clean themselves, and eat food.

She swallows and thinks the same as Howie, that she wants nothing more than to sleep in a bath of ice or inside a refrigerated truck on a cold mattress with Clarence. She just can't cool down. It's her insides. They've been baked through.

'How the hell are we still alive?' she asks.

Marcy glances at her. Howie and Reginald do the same from Paula voicing something she'd never say in front of the lads. Not from any sense of false bravado, but because confidence is a fragile thing, and the leaders can't show that the fear gets to them as much as everyone else.

'We know why,' Reginald says. Still wearing a white shirt and tie, albeit the shirt doesn't look white at all now. Not after the day they had yesterday.

The thirtieth day in the new world, and that milestone seared itself into their minds with a blistering non-stop day of war and butchery.

A day of moving swiftly from battle to battle. Chasing hordes and culling the numbers.

A day of intensity, during which they only stopped long enough to gulp water and eat high-energy snack bars.

A day in which Charlie grappled with the mixed

messages coming from Cookey, and Maddox and Booker forged a new friendship.

A day in which Howie and Henry battled each other and their own egos. Each wanting to lead. Each refusing to submit to the other's will.

Reginald knew that unless that situation was resolved, it would fester and disrupt the harmony of the pack. Which wasn't a thing Reginald wanted at all because that didn't suit Reginald's plans. Which were, of course, *the actual plans*. That being because Reginald was *the actual boss*. Not that he said that out loud, of course.

Reginald's plan was to not only continue to cull the numbers – which Reginald knew was vital *before releasing the panacea,* but also to force Henry and Howie into such a shit sandwich, they'd have to work together to survive. Or, of course, they'd all die trying. But then, you can't make an omelette without cracking a few eggs. Not that Reginald was in anyway experienced in omelette making, or indeed, any other egg-based meals.

But either way, Reginald's *Churchill* speech worked, and no sooner than later, they were all whipped up and sent off into Gatwick airport, with Henry working with Paula to extract the survivors in the terminals, while Howie went and picked a fight. That being their normal, standard go-to method of fighting hordes.

Which swiftly came undone because they'd never been so bloody stupid as to take on fifty thousand infected, made up from two control points on flat, open ground with no hard cover or landscape options to force bottlenecks or, indeed, any other tactical methods.

Things went south quickly. Henry and Paula led their team out of the terminal to give aid, but even that didn't help.

In the end, it got so bad that Howie did what any self-respecting leader of vagabonds would do in such a deadly situation. *He deployed Dave.*

Who promptly blew everything up.

Silos. Fuel trucks. Planes. Pipes.

Day turned to night. Buildings were ripped apart. The terminals were destroyed. Fire engines were lifted off the ground and sent hurtling through the air, and aircraft wheels were turned into missiles. Howie and Henry got everyone hunkered down behind the only brick building they could find, but even that was blown apart.

It was hell on earth.

Thousands were killed instantly.

But it wasn't enough, and when the smoke cleared, two new control points emerged, and the frenzied hordes instantly pressed their attack.

It grew desperate.

Cookey was taken down. Charlie. Danny. Mo Mo. Tappy got trapped and only survived when the Saxon rolled over her, convincing her the ghost of her father had somehow made it move. Maddox and Booker dragged her free and went to the others, and they too got taken down. Nick. Paula. Carmen. There were too many coming at them from all sides at once – and when Clarence was taken off his feet, the largest and strongest of them all, they all feared it was over.

Reginald yelled in frustration. Trapped in his van, with a horde outside. They were done. It was over.

Until Marcy arrived with an army of her own. Driving tanks and flying old fighter jets into the fray.

It turned the battle, but Joan got trapped at the top of the air-traffic control tower. None could reach her.

'You know what to do, Marcy.' Joan said into the radio.

Marcy refused. She couldn't do it. *'I'm okay with this,'* Joan said. She'd killed children in the throes of turning. She watched them in her scope, then put a round in each of them to end the suffering.

Marcy did what had to be done and made the fighter jets fly into the tower with an explosion of jet-fuel that killed thousands of infected scaling the sides.

That act, and the support given by Tilda Tanners from Christ's Hospital, which as Cookey said was confusing AF because it wasn't a hospital at all but a school for posh kids. But it was also a posh school with its own military cadet academy, which included an armoury – and it was those posh kids, trained and led by former Captain Tilda Tanners, who arrived on the field of battle in an armoured school bus to take on the rest of the infected, thereby, saving Howie and his team.

Or as Reginald noted, Howie *and* Henry's team.

Because they'd all felt it in the battle.

They felt Henry's energy joining the pack. They felt him absorb into that intangible thing they have between them. And they felt that same energy that Howie had that drove them to fight as one also came from Henry. The same power. The same unbreakable will.

Except, where Howie was wildly violent, Henry was focussed and controlled.

Either way. Reginald's plan worked. Howie accepted Henry. Henry accepted Howie.

But was it worth it?

They lost Joan.

Clarence lost his hand. Danny lost fingers. Cookey might have lost an eye. Mo had half of one ear torn away. They're all cut to bits and almost out of ammunition. Axes broke. Knives were dropped. Pistols lost. Only the Saxon is running properly.

Was it worth it?

Reginald sits in that rumbling, creaking, vibrating van and feels the rain on his face, coming inside from the broken sliding door held open by a bungee cord. His clothes torn and filthy. His tie pulled down. His sleeves rolled up. His battle swatter still gripped in his hand, and Howie turns once more to look at him. Seemingly knowing the question hanging in the air.

Was it worth it?

They both know the answer.

Yes.

Because this is the game, and these are the rules, and they *all* go in knowing that.

And besides, they took out more than fifty thousand infected and saved hundreds of people. And that was just at the end of the day. They saved scores more people and killed thousands more infected throughout the day.

So, yes. It was fucking worth it.

Every pure second of hell they endured was worth it.

But that heat.

My god, that was something else, and that blaze of energy in Howie's eyes seems to fade as he turns back to the grey world outside as the SUV follows the van that follows the Saxon once more leading the way.

Tappy driving her. Her nose broken. Her eyes swollen and purple. Her arms bitten, clawed, and marked, but she's no different to everyone else.

Meredith beside her. The front passenger seat now hers, although in fairness, she does have a piece of Clarence with her.

'Gross,' Tappy says, glancing at the dismembered hand

still in her mouth as Meredith gives a low growl at Tappy daring to look at it.

Don't look. Mine.

'Okay, okay,' Tappy says.

The rest behind them, in the back. Rocking gently to the motion of the Saxon. Charlie next to Cookey. She looks at the bandages wrapped around his head and held together by gaffer tape to protect his injured eye and prays that he hasn't lost it. She loves his blue eyes. She loves seeing them and when they look at her, and right now, she'd give one of her own for Cookey to keep both of his.

They all think the same. Blowers. Tappy. Nick. Even the elders in the van, and Henry's team at the rear.

Cookey is almost defined by his eyes. The way they twinkle and shine. The nearly ever-present show of play and humour pouring from his very being.

Mo's grin. Danny's speed. Dave's skill. Clarence's size. Nick's abilities to make things work. The unkillable nature of Simon Blowers. Tappy's driving. Charlie's bond with Jess. Roy's skill with his bow. Reginald's brain They all have something, and Cookey has his eyes.

'You okay?' she asks again.

His mouth flickers with a hint of a smile. 'I'll get a disabled badge like Blowers now,' he says as Blowers gives him a middle finger but stays silent. A tapestry of injuries, the same as Howie. His ruined eye now exposed. He did cover it with a patch, but it slipped in the heat and got lost in that almighty melee.

The one in which Charlie got cut to pieces again, and Danny lost two fingers, and Mo's ear got ripped off.

'You two alright?' Blowers asks, looking down to the two young lads at the back doors. They both nod, as exhausted and broken as everyone else. Everyone except Blowers, that is. Cos, honestly? Danny and Mo are not even sure Sergeant Blowers actually feels pain. Danny lost fingers, and Mo half an ear, but Blowers lost fingers, an eye, and whole chunks of his body protecting Mads delivering that baby *at the same time*. And he died for like, literally five minutes and still got back up, and killed more infected with his bare hands. He literally did that. Fact.

'He's like Chuck Norris,' Danny told Mo. 'Even death is scared of him.'

They both stare in awe at their sergeant, acting like literally nothing happened while everyone else groans and clutches their wounds.

'Wake up,' Maddox says as he kicks Booker's foot. The lad opens one eye with a tired grin and flicks a middle finger in the same way Blowers did to Cookey.

A new friendship between them. Maddox Doku and Alan Booker. Booker was one of the lads through and through and fought with Howie and the others at the battle for Salisbury, but then he went off, and when he came back, the dynamics had shifted.

The lads still accepted him, but old faces were gone, and new faces had joined, and Booker found himself not quite within the same internal faction of the greater tribe that he once was.

Which is how Maddox has always felt, in the old life and now in this one, and as they waged war throughout the day of days yesterday, they seemed to find each other and found themselves teaming up.

Maddox didn't trust Booker one bit before they became pals. There was something wrong about him, and Maddox kept following Booker and putting him under a spotlight while searching every word Booker said for hidden meaning.

Now Maddox realises he was being paranoid and looking for mysteries and conspiracies as a reaction to not having a position of leadership. Maddox was in charge in his old compound. Then again, in the fort. But he fucked it up.

Whatever. He's not even bothered.

Mind you, Frank mentioned something about training him yesterday when they stopped at that shopping centre when Marcy sneezed on that guy, and there was almost a big fight between Henry and Howie.

It's weird, because to everyone else, that confrontation kinda sorted all the issues out, and everyone else got on with it, but Henry and Howie still had to keep measuring their dicks.

Maddox snorts at the thought while figuring Reginald is probably the proper boss, without Howie and Henry even noticing. They always do what Reginald wants, and they go where Reginald plans for them to go.

How is that *not* being the boss?

But again. Whatever. He's not even bothered and closes his eyes, soaked through and hurting from too many injuries. Desperately hungry and needing sleep. A jab at his foot. He opens his eyes to see Booker winking and mouthing *wake up*. The energy still flowing between them, even now.

But still.

That heat.

That was something else, and neither Maddox or Booker, or any of the others feel they'll be cold again. All of them feeling the same. Like they were baked alive.

'Not far now,' Tappy calls from the front.

Grunts of relief. They're almost back at Camber. Back to the place they've come to know as home. They'll clean the weapons and make-ready. Clean themselves, then eat, and sleep, preferably on a bed of ice.

It's not just them that feels that way.

Had the world been functioning, the weather satellites would have transmitted data and images to clever people working in offices who would have created reports that would have been distributed to news agencies everywhere, all of whom would broadcast images of the whole planet seemingly experiencing a heatwave at the same time.

But the world is not functioning, and those satellites, although still recording, are mostly crashing back to Earth, having been sucked into the planet's gravitational pull.

Most of them burn up in the atmosphere on re-entry. A few don't and have been seen, the world over, streaking through the sky with golden tails.

Howie saw them and thought one would land on their heads. Because, why wouldn't it? They're shit magnets.

Henry told him the chances were so remote they weren't even worth considering.

Howie wasn't so sure, although he did accept the planet is a very big place, and that for the most part, satellites are really quite small, but obviously, that's only the ones they know about, and there are plenty that people don't know about.

Like the US government's covert and formally hidden SilentBlack spy satellite, for instance. It's still functioning and capturing images to transmit back to now empty offices, devoid of clever people, most of whom are no longer very clever at all, given that they're running around, trying to bite people.

Even as it hits the edge of the atmosphere, and the enormous solar wings get torn off and burnt to ash in seconds, the SilentBlack satellite keeps recording as it tumbles and twists, and spins, and falls.

But then, the satellite was constructed to withstand an interstellar missile strike from Russia or China, or any other number of state operators that had grudges against the western world – and so, while it does heat up, and bits do fly off, the bulk of it remains intact– until suddenly, it's hurtling through the highest parts of the sky. Still reading the planet below. Seeing fires and tower blocks torn down in New York, all around Central Park now fortified and held by people of different colours and creeds that hated each other in the old world but now live and fight, and die side by side.

And the SilentBlack spy satellite flies on in a streak of golden heat over the Atlantic ocean. Seeing cargo ships and tankers smashed into the coast. Others anchored out to sea, with the people inside holding revolutions of their own to overthrow despotic captains. War and death. Always war and death.

On and on the satellite flies. Over the deepest parts of the ocean where the whales sing their songs of a species now fallen and the great silence coming back to their waters where the fish stocks are already increasing.

On and on the satellite flies. Ireland below. Green and lush. The cities burning. The towns fallen. The Protestants and Catholics took arms against each other. War and death. Always war and death. But those signs were torn down, and new leaders emerged. Leaders with no loyalty to any version of any God.

The north coast of England. The cities and towns the same as all the others. Fires burning, and the signs of great violence seen everywhere. But compounds glimpsed. Places where the people rushed to hold ground. While the countryside seems very green and very vast, broken only by isolated dwellings and farms. A single house spotted in the distance. Miles from anything else. A bright red fire engine in the garden next to a large inflatable pool.

The satellite flies on. Liverpool in the distance. More smoking ruins. Chester Castle. People streaming inside, but it's a glimpse only through the low clouds disgorging rain, and the satellite flies on over the countryside. Dropping down into the clouds where the moisture within turns to steam on contact with the ultra-hot surface.

Then it's out and free, and flying over the south of England.

A tiny island off the coast, distinct from the air because of the giant wall made from different coloured metal containers.

Smoke billowing from Gatwick. Fires still raging, and from the air the epicentre of the blast is clear, with a radius of broken buildings getting less damaged as it spreads out. The explosions wrought by Dave when he blew the fuel silos. The explosions that turned day into night and killed tens of thousands of infected within a split-second, and enabled the clan of survivors to escape once more.

Clambering into their vehicles and setting out in the pouring rain and pitch-dark of night to drive south. Back to the place they've come to call home. Back to the place where they can tend their many terrible injuries and heal from the heat and terror of the battles they endured.

Back to Camber Airstrip. A small grass runway for light aircraft on a flat section of coastline next to the steep cliffs overlooking the seas of the English Channel.

Three vehicles inching slowly along. Led by the squat and stocky Saxon at the front. Roy's van and Henry's SUV behind.

They come to a stop. The doors open, and they clamber out, nearly as broken and damaged as the vehicles. All of them hurt. All of them weary to the bone. Covered in grime and filth that clogs the pores of their skin. Clothing torn and blackened. The rain falling hard. Soaking their heads and faces while they groan inwardly at the thought of having to clean weapons and make-ready *before* they can eat and sleep.

Clarence feels it too. But he's one of the elders, and so he summons the resolve needed to show leadership as he blinks up at the sky, and the streak of golden light coming in low and fast like a missile.

The beat of a heart.

The blink of an eye, and time enough to only shout one word.

'COVER!'

He turns fast while giving warning. Going in hard like a rugby player. Driving with his legs into Paula and Danny, and Mo, scooping them up into Tappy and Nick, and Charlie. A concertina of human forms being compressed as Clarence slams them all down.

Henry shouts and dives for cover. Reginald dives into the van. Frank, Carmen, and Bash hit the ground. Roy, Maddox, and Booker diving away as the satellite slams into the clubhouse.

It's Gatwick all over again, with bricks and chunks of buildings hitting the vehicles, with Henry's SUV hit so hard it spins around and around while sliding over the muddy grass.

They feel the impact too. The awful, gut-wrenching boom and thud from the satellite striking the ground. Making it vibrate and shake. The small air-traffic control tower blows out so fast that bricks sail over the edge of the cliff.

What a thing to see. The power of it. The speed of it.

Howie does the same as everyone else and buries his head in his arms while hunkering down within the mass of bodies, and only after the initial impact does he risk a glance to see the building exploding out and the satellite breaking up as it bounces and careens off, with flames already blazing from the intense heat it carried down.

A harsh stench in the air.

Chemicals. Burnt metal and ceramics. Howie peers over to Henry, prone in the rain-slicked mud, staring in shocked awe.

'What did I bloody say!' Howie shouts. 'We are literally shit magnets.'

Henry doesn't quite know what to say and stares back at the smouldering ruins of Camber clubhouse and tower while figuring they'll need to find somewhere else. 'Suggest we –,' he starts to say but cuts off as they all snap their heads up to scores of rabbits bounding past as though fleeing for their lives.

'What the,' Howie says at the sight of Meredith cocking her head over while staring at the ground in a way none of them have seen before.

Bashir frowns and turns to look at the cliff edge, lost in the dark and pelting rain. Then he remembers the fissures and turns to see one nearby. A long, thin rent in the earth where the moisture has been pulled out, causing big cracks to form. Not just here either. Every field and meadow have them in this area from the prolonged heat.

He used to see them before in Afghanistan when it went through drought. 'How high is that cliff?' he asks in his native tongue.

'The cliff?' Mo relays. 'He wants to know how high the cliff is.'

'Why does he want to know that?' Paula asks but gets cut off by Bashir speaking urgently.

'He really wants to know,' Mo says.

'Tell him it's about thirty metres high,' Nick says as Bashir blinks at him, understanding the words before scrabbling to his feet while shouting a warning in broken English.

'Bug out! Bug out!'

They burst for the vehicles, with none of them grasping why as yet more rabbits bound past. Foxes with them. Badgers seen running nearby. Birds in flight. Crying out. All of them heading in the same direction and away from the edge of the cliff.

Howie's team aim for the Saxon and Roy's van. Henry's team for the SUV. Meredith barks sudden and harsh, and the animals steaming past go faster. A dull sucking sound reaches them over the sound of the rain. A sudden shift in the earth beneath their feet. A weird feeling of sliding.

'It's giving way!' Henry calls, realising what Bashir meant. He runs for his vehicle only to see the SUV sliding away as though gently pulled across ice. Henry blinks at the sight and for a second thinks to run after it, but the fissure opens sudden and wide. A gaping rent in the earth with a wet sucking sound as the holes in the bone-dry earth fill with water and get wider, and split the ground.

A shout. A yell. The cliff gives way. Tearing metres of earth with it. Making them all feel the drop in height, and Henry watches the SUV drop out of sight as the edge of the earth comes at them.

'The van!' someone yells as they snatch a glimpse of Roy's van turning sharply as the ground starts giving way, making it twist sharply, with the horse box still attached to the back with Jess inside. Kicking the back door as the trailer bucks and slides in the mud.

Charlie dives for the closed ramp, but the ground heaves and pulls the van and the horse box away and out of reach. Screams and yells sound out. Everything happening in an instant. Tappy already in the Saxon, powering on to get traction to get away from the crumbling edge rapidly giving away, with tonnes of mud collapsing down thirty metres to the rock and shingle beach below.

Charlie grunts and dives for it. Using the mud to slide into the back of the trailer with a bone-crunching crack as her shin strikes the hard metal ledge. She clings on to it, kicking at the bolt stuck in its housing from the trailer buckling and twisting. Jess inside. Kicking with panic as she feels the trailer tilting over. The van drops another foot. The muddy edge giving way.

'Charlie!' Cookey yells, diving after her. Getting to her side, with both of them booting at the bolt. Making it shift a millimetre at a time. 'CLARENCE!' Cookey screams the big man's name. Knowing they can't shift it.

He comes running. All six feet six of him sprinting, then diving to slide with a grim look as Cookey pulls Charlie away, and Clarence hits the back of the sliding trailer with a thud. He grips on and yells, and brings his boot up to kick and kick, and kick at that fucking bolt. Tearing the fitting out. Screaming with berserker fury. Jess inside doing the same. The van sliding. The trailer tilting.

One last kick from Clarence, but the trailer yanks away from him and starts dropping as Jess uses both back legs to slam into the ramp from the inside, prising the last bolt from the frame. The ramp drops, almost hitting Clarence who tries to run but slips, and slides and, narrowly misses Jess running out. Her hooves slipping and sliding. Not getting traction. Her eyes rolling with fear.

Charlie grabs her reins and heaves to keep topside of the crumbling cliff edge. Maddox and Booker with her. The lads running in. Carmen. Henry. Frank. Clarence runs into Jess's side, heaving with his shoulder to get her away from the edge as his own feet start slipping over.

'COME ON, JESS!' Charlie roars as Clarence grits his teeth and squats with every ounce of strength to give Jess enough lift to get her back feet out of the mud as she gains traction with a sudden burst that makes the others fly back from the pressure releasing in the reins.

A split-second to gasp, but the ground is still heaving, and the edge is still crumbling. They scrabble away, crying out in fear and shock as the van pivots and spins around like it's sliding on ice, presenting the passenger side as the horse trailer whips around and slams over onto its side. The front of the van now lower than the back, and the whole thing sliding fast towards the crumbling edge.

And in that second, they gain sight of the inside of the van and Reginald, still inside trying to heave his way out against the van tilting away. He shouts and dives, but the front drops lower, and that bungee cord holding the broken sliding door open snaps and pings back, slamming into Reginald's hand gripping the frame like a whip, making him yell as the door slams shut and the van drops out of sight. The horse trailer disappearing with it.

'NO!' Howie screams and tries to run for the edge, Clarence grabbing his arm to throw him back. Howie rallies and tries again, but Frank grabs and heaves him away.

'It's thirty metres, you bloody idiot!' Frank yells. 'GET IN! GET IN!' he screams at the others. Yelling at them to get into the Saxon as Tappy powers on and off and heaves the wheel hard left and right to keep traction. Moving forward a foot at a time to keep away from the edge of the cliff.

'We can't leave him!' Howie shouts, but the noise is too great. The Saxon's engine. The roaring fires within the clubhouse, and the almighty sucking sounds of the cliff edge tearing away, and the rumble of rocks and mud slamming down the cliff to the bottom.

The SUV with it.

The van too.

With Reginald inside.

2

Darkness.

Darkness absolute.

But not silence, and it's the noises that wake him up to an intense pain in his skull that pulses harder when he gasps out loud – except the sound isn't it.

It's muted and strange. Which suggests the sound waves aren't moving as they normally would. Nor is he able to see any light. He clamps his eyes closed, then opens them again. No change. Nothing at all.

Another noise drifts over.

A dull thud.

He snaps his head over with a fresh wave of nausea, and it takes seconds of breathing in and out to fight the sense of panic inside.

He was in the van.

The van went off the cliff.

'Oh dear,' he whispers. Hearing that dull sound that makes him realise the van is buried under tonnes of mud which has created the soundproofed walls. Which in turn means that shouting for help is completely useless. And who would he shout for? They all saw him sliding off the cliff edge as the door slammed shut.

What an awful feeling that was. That sudden shift in gravity as the van fell, which in turn caused him to become weightless, albeit, only for a second or so before he hit the bottom, at which point he ceased to be weightless and slammed into the side. Or the back. Which he can't tell because he can't see a blasted thing.

He shifts position. Thinking to grope around and gain a sense of his position in relation to the vehicle around him, but the sudden sharp bloom of intense pain in his left hand makes him gasp and stop.

He brings it up to his face, but he can't see a thing. Why do his fingers hurt so much? Are they broken? He tries to move them, but something isn't right. He brings his right hand up to grope at his left and gasps once more at the feel of the hot wet sticky blood on the stumps where his fingers used to be.

His fingers that were severed off when the sliding door slammed shut.

'Oh dear,' he whimpers again and sags back as the whole van seems to shift and groan with a sensation of sliding. A crashing sound outside. More mud hitting the van walls. The windscreen fractures. He can hear it. The walls start buckling, and he squeezes his eyes shut, ready for the walls or the door, or the windscreen to give way and the cloying wet mud to crush him to death.

3

It seems to last for eternity.

The Saxon powering on and away from the ruins of Camber Clubhouse, with Jess galloping at their side. Charlie on her back, crouched low, with the rain pelting her face. Everyone else crammed and slammed in the back of the Saxon. Bodies on top of bodies, and Clarence clinging to the back of the open doors with his one good hand while Maddox and Nick hold his belt from the inside to stop him falling away.

A feeling of panic inside all of them at seeing Reginald drop. The most awful of sensations that something just went so terribly wrong so terribly fast.

But it's all they can do to hold on and bounce, and rock, and slam into each other while Tappy drives like a demon. Powering on adjacent to the cliff falling away in huge chunks, tens of metres in width and depth. Hundreds of tonnes at a time crashing down. The very earth itself seeming to break apart.

Weeks of relentless heat and storms. Droughts. Flash floods. The old world is changing. The new world is here.

Landscapes are changing, and all they can do is keep going and hope to hell they don't get pulled down.

Tappy snaps her head left, seeing the cliff just feet away, then spots the crack in the ground. Another fissure opening fast and stretching away faster than she can drive. She punches power while steering right. Charlie sees the motion and leans as Jess veers away and leaps a fence. Sailing high through the air to land in the surface water pouring over the hard-baked ground.

A crunch of wood, and the Saxon smashes through that same fence and enters the furrowed field. Bouncing over the lanes made by tractors tilling and sowing the soil.

Shouts in the back. Ribs being hurt. Bones being crunched. Pain on top of agony.

Another deep, long, thunderous sound from behind as Clarence twists to see a massive swathe of cliff giving way at once as the Saxon bounces over the field and smashes through a hedge on the other side, forming a hole for Jess to get through before hitting the motorway, and aquaplaning for long metres on the surface water.

'BRACE!' Tappy yells. Unable to power on or steer. She angles the wheel and powers on and off, feeling the loss of traction. Waiting for the tyres to bite the ground. A jolt as they slam into the metal railing of the central reservation and send it pinging off as they travel through and slide across the next lane.

The tyres grip. The Saxon jinks hard, sending everyone in the back over to the left as Tappy powers on. 'Is it safe to stop?' she yells, unable to see behind from the press of bodies.

Clarence twists. Seeing the cliff edge back over the hedge they went through now at least two hundred metres away.

'Yes!' he shouts, and the Saxon slows to a stop, with Clarence dropping away and reaching in with his one good hand to help the others out. All of them dropping into the rain. Bent over and gasping for air. Fresh cuts. Fresh wounds. Fresh bruises.

'We've got to go back,' Howie says the very second he gets out.

'Going back to that cliff is suicide, nipper,' Frank says.

'We can't just fucking leave him!'

'Howie, we can't get down that cliff,' Henry says.

'I fucking can!'

'Howie!' Frank shouts, grabbing at his arm as Howie tries to pull away and thinks to run back and scale the cliff. 'We've got to think! Get a grip!'

Sharp words from a hard man that makes Howie stop and glare at Frank with that dark fury blazing in his eyes, but Howie heeds the words. His mind in turmoil. His heart gripped with panic at the thought of Reginald hurt and alone.

'We can't just stand here,' Blowers says. 'Nick, how do we get down that cliff?'

'Ropes?' Nick asks.

'LISTEN!' Henry shouts with a sharp rebuke, sensing their loyalty to Reginald and knowing they won't stop until they get to him. 'Going down that cliff is suicide.'

'Fuck's sake!' Cookey says.

'We can't do nothing,' Blowers snaps.

'Major Henry is talking!' Dave shouts them down. Gaining compliance.

'Going *down* the cliff is suicide,' Henry says, glaring at them all. 'We are not lemmings. We don't run to our deaths in panic. Grip yourselves. We think, and we plan, and we get it right first time. Right. What did we see?'

'Reggie in the van,' Cookey says.

'Correct. Reginald was *inside* the van. The door slammed shut. Yes? Did anyone see that?' Henry asks.

Nods and murmurs. 'I saw that,' Charlie says. 'I was staring right at him.'

'Concurred,' Carmen says. Looking stricken to the core as she replays that last split-second of seeing the look of shock on Reginald's face as the bungee hit him, and the door slammed shut at the exact time the van slipped away.

'Good. That means Reginald is inside,' Henry says.

'But the door's fucked,' Nick adds.

'But it closed, and unless the van twisted in mid-air, which is not likely, then I suggest the door remained closed,' Henry says. Radiating calmness as the others stand in the rain. Grim-faced, with chests heaving.

'But that was a big drop,' Roy says.

'Roy!' Carmen snaps.

'What? It was a big drop.'

'I will fucking deck you,' Carmen snarls, making him flinch.

'Read the room, you idiot,' Marcy says.

'What room? And it was a big drop!'

'Is it going to stop us trying to reach him?' Carmen demands, turning on Roy in an instant. Jabbing a hand into his chest. Driving him back.

'Of course not.'

'Then why say it? Why, Roy? WHY?'

'Carmen! Stand down,' Henry orders.

'Don't tell me what to do, Henry.'

'Okay. Easy,' Paula says, grabbing her arm to pull her away. 'Just stand with me. We'll get to him. Listen to me. All of you. We'll find a way, but screaming and shouting at each other won't help Reginald. So, Roy? Unless it's constructive, please shut the fuck up.'

'I was just saying.'

'I will fucking shoot you!' Carmen snaps with a sudden flash of rage that makes Roy finally fall silent.

'The van is armoured,' Henry adds quickly. 'The walls are solid, and the frame is strong, so yes, it *was* a big drop, but it also, hopefully, wasn't a sheer drop. It would have fallen *with* the cliff which would have lessened the speed, *and* hopefully, the impact at the base.'

Roy grimaces. Figuring even the van couldn't withstand hundreds of tonnes of rocks and mud on top of it, but this time he keeps his mouth shut.

'How do we get to it?' Howie asks, looking to Roy and Nick, then to Tappy. The engineers. The doers.

'Henry's right. We can't go down that cliff,' Roy says. 'Even with ropes. It's too unstable.'

'What *can* we do?' Howie asks.

'Well, we'd have to go in from the beach,' Roy says as the first pulse of hope spreads out.

'We need a boat, then. Where from? Anyone? Come on! Speak up.'

'There's a harbour at Eastbourne,' Paula says. 'That's not far. And it's got a lifeboat station. We can use that.'

'Let's do it,' Howie says.

'Wait!' Henry calls as they start to burst away. 'Is Eastbourne clear?'

'Clear of what?' Howie asks.

'Have you cleared it? The infected?' Henry asks as Howie frowns, then flushes with dark rage again.

'We haven't cleared it,' Clarence says.

'I'll fucking get through it,' Howie says.

'Howie! We don't have ammunition to fight through,' Henry says.

'We've got barely one mag for each rifle,' Frank adds. 'Two mags for each sidearm, and they're useless unless you can get a headshot up close.'

'Which none of us can do,' Paula says. 'Apart from Dave.'

'We can't just fucking stand here with our thumbs up our arses!' Howie shouts.

'We think. We plan. We succeed,' Henry says calmly as Howie looks ready to shout in temper again. 'I am on your side, Howie. Taking a moment to plan means we don't lose further lives.'

Howie swallows the anger. Henry is right.

'Listen. If he's dead, then he's dead,' Frank says bluntly. 'But if he's alive, then leaping off cliffs ain't gonna help him. We think. We plan. We succeed. We do not panic. Right, let's have a hot brief. Eastbourne is a big town. If that's not cleared, then we can't risk trying to punch through. What's south along the coast from Eastbourne?'

'Beachy head,' Roy says. 'But that region has *really* big cliffs, and that's the wrong direction from Camber. We need to go north *up* the coast.'

'Okay, next harbour north up the coast from Eastbourne is what? Hastings?'

'Hastings,' a few of them say.

'Cleared?' Henry asks.

Paula shakes her head.

'Alright. Stay calm,' Frank says as the mutters threaten to get louder.

'They might be empty,' Howie says. 'We've been fighting hordes around here for a month. They might have drawn out to attack us. That might have been them at Gatwick.'

'And if ifs and buts were candies and nuts, I'd get a blowjob,' Frank says.

'We *must* consider all eventualities,' Henry adds. 'And we won't know until we go in, at which point we get surrounded, and we cannot get out, and that leaves Reginald stranded.'

'Okay,' Howie says, knowing every word Henry and Frank says makes sense. 'We need a small, quiet harbour, then?'

Silence as they all think.

'Oh god. What's wrong with me. Idiot!' Roy says, palming his own forehead. 'Rye!'

'Rye,' Frank says as Henry nods quickly.

'That's perfect,' Henry says. 'Small village. Big harbour.'

'And it's closer to Camber,' Roy adds. 'Camber town is right next to it, but the airstrip is a few miles up the coast.'

'It's not far, then?' Marcy asks.

'No, really close,' Roy says. 'Sorry, guys. I should have thought of it.'

Half of them wanted to swing punches at Roy a few seconds ago, now they tell him not to be hard on himself as the energy spikes and flows in the charged dynamics.

'Rye it is,' Henry says. 'Right. Listen in. The *mission objective* is to reach Rye harbour and secure a vessel to get to the beach area below Camber airstrip. Is that understood?'

Mo translates quietly, with Bashir nodding. Not knowing the names or places but grasping the mission at hand.

Howie listens in. Realising how it makes a difference to

speak it out in simple terms that everyone can understand, and more importantly, it gives them all a mission objective to focus on and thereby reduces the feel of panic welling up inside.

'We need to consider what *type* of vessel will be suitable,' Henry adds to more than a few frowns. 'What type of beach is it? How do we get from the boat to the beach? Do we need tools when we arrive? Where will we get those from? Do we need ropes or chains? We think. We plan. We succeed.'

'Engineers,' Howie says, looking to Nick, Tappy, and Roy.

'The van and the four-wheel drive went over the cliff with *a lot* of mud,' Nick says. 'And more mud fell after. So, the chances are it's buried. We'll need spades and shovels. Pickaxes too, in case we need to break through rocks or stones. Yeah, so we'll need a builder's merchant or even a DIY store.'

'We'll find one on the way through,' Henry says. 'You three, keep planning. Everyone else, stay calm. Stay grounded. We *will* get to Reginald. Mr Howie, you can give the order to move out.'

'Yes, Major,' Howie says without hesitation. 'Mads, you drive.'

'Eh? Why?' Tappy asks.

'Do not question Mr Howie!' Dave says.

'There's too many of us, Tappy,' Howie says. 'Clarence will go up front with Mads as they're the two biggest. Everyone else bundle in. Tappy and Roy, stay close to Nick and keep planning what we might need to reach Reginald.'

'Cookey, get on Jess with me,' Charlie says.

'Will Reggie be able to breath?' Danny asks with a look

of horror at the thought of being trapped under a mountain of mud.

'For one person in that van, yes,' Nick says confidently. 'And Reggie's smart. He'll know not to panic and waste air.

4

'Oh god! Oh god! Oh god!' Reginald says, trapped in the van in the middle of a panic attack. 'My fingers! They're all shorn off.'

He blusters and gasps, and then wonders why on earth he used the word *shorn* in such a way. Why not *severed*? Or he could have just said they were *cut off*. At which point he realises he's then panicking at the words he's using *about* panicking over his shorn off fingers.

'Damn it!' he used shorn again, and he gasps and sucks air in, and blows it out, and then convinces himself he can actually feel his fingers wriggling on his left hand and gropes at it again, only to yelp at the pain while realising he was right the first time because they are most definitely shorn off.

'Cut!' he snaps at himself. 'Cut off. Ah yes, but shorn does also fit the situation. Yes. Yes, it does, Reginald. *So how about you stop flapping,* as Joan would say, *and start using that brain of yours, and wasting air, you silly, little man.*'

Joan's voice in his mind. He remembers her at the top of

the air traffic control tower at Gatwick, telling Marcy to just go ahead and kill her while as calm as a anything.

It does the job. He regains composure. His breathing easing down. Wet mud can easily create an air-tight seal, and if the windows or panels, or that broken sliding door don't give in, there's every chance he'll suffocate to death.

But then, the inside of the van held some decent volume, which means that if he's careful and doesn't hyperventilate, he can breathe for a good time yet.

See. Now you're thinking properly, Reginald, Joan tells him in his mind as the van shifts and seems to drop another foot or so, and he clamps his eyes closed at the world beyond the walls thundering down, with every sound now magnified in the darkness.

The panels bending in. The metal warping.

The windscreen fracturing with more cracks.

Wait.

The windscreen.

He can hear it.

He cranes his head to listen.

It's above him.

Which means the back of the van is behind him, and the van is facing up.

And now you've gained your place and position.

He feels rather pleased with himself for a second until the van drops another foot with more mud or rocks slamming into the sides with an awful scraping sound as something gives way.

What was that?

It sounded like the windscreen.

But the windscreen is thick and solid, and designed to withstand gunfire.

He frowns. Realising that the noise isn't the windscreen cracking, but the whole blasted thing sliding inwards.

Then the scraping stops, and he holds still as wet mud hits his face.

Wet mud falling down from above.

5

They go in on the Folkestone Road towards Rye, passing the junction to Camber Road, leading to Camber town.

Maddox driving. Clarence in the front. Everyone else apart from Charlie and Cookey crammed in the back, shoulder to shoulder on the bench seats or standing in the middle.

A rumble of distant thunder above the low clouds makes Howie stare out the open back doors to the rain still falling. Making the world beyond the Saxon look grey and dark. The pace feels slow too. Painfully slow, but they don't have a horse box trailer which means going slow enough for Jess to keep pace.

Frustration inside. A sense of needing to rush and get there. That glimpse trapped in his mind, the same as everyone else. The look on Reginald's face when the bungee whipped his right hand and loosened his grip, preventing him from heaving himself out and clear as the door slammed shut, and the van dropped away.

Is he alive? Is Reginald alive?

Reginald is a part of the hive mind they have. Surely they would feel it if he died, but there was so much going on, and right then that hive mind thing wasn't active or turned on, or whatever it's called when they can all feel each other.

All he can do is pray that Reginald is still alive. Then Howie remembers he hates God on a molecular level and thinks God can fuck himself or herself, or itself, then immediately worries that by insulting God he'll cause the death of Reginald.

He rubs his face and groans.

Why is this even happening?

They saved people at Gatwick, with one of their own dying in the process. Haven't they done enough now? Haven't they *given* enough?

He looks forward out the windscreen and curses at the slow pace, and breathes the hot steamed air caused by too many wet bodies crammed in together.

But still. It's got to be better than being trapped in a van, slowly being crushed by tonnes of mud.

'Fuck's sake, come on,' Carmen snaps under her breath, making Howie look over to her standing in the middle the same as him. Her face a mask of intense frustration and worry. He hasn't seen Carmen like that before, and she went for Roy back on the road.

But then, everyone loves Reginald, and the thought of him being alone and dying slowly, or being crushed while hurt has made them all silent and brooding.

'Okay. Shovels, spades, chains, ropes, pickaxes… And any other digging and groundwork tools we can find,' Tappy says, scribbling it down on a pad taken from Paula. 'And we need to think what kind of boat we need.'

'Man. We might just have to take what we can find,' Nick says. 'Lifeboat would be good.'

'But what if it's housed up that big ramp thing?' Paula asks. 'Doesn't it need power to launch? Like electricity or something.'

'That's a very good point,' Tappy says.

'I'll find a workaround,' Nick says. 'But we need something shallow that can get in close to the beach. I mean, it's not windy so the sea should be calm.'

'I just heard thunder,' Howie says from the back doors. 'But it's not windy yet.'

'Do we know anything about the tides?' Tappy asks.

'Strong tides around here,' Roy says. 'We'll just have to hope they're not pulling us out or down or... I don't know.'

'We'll get to him,' Carmen says out loud, making everyone look at her. 'If I have to swim, I'll fucking get to him.'

Henry frowns. Not used to hearing Carmen swear or seeing that level of intensity pouring from her either. But then, Reginald *is* very popular. Henry can feel it himself. That need to be there right now. His hand clenches at his side. The knuckles cracking and turning white, and like everyone else, he wishes they'd go faster.

Outside in the rain, Cookey winces on the horse. Not used to the discomfort of being in a saddle. The rain pelting his face. Blurring the vision in his eye and making the bandage wrapped around his head grow soggy and start drooping. He tries to tug it up, but Charlie tells him she can't see and to drop his arm.

Thunder above makes Jess snort and twitch, and the rain seems to come down harder, obscuring the view.

Something looms on the left. Then, on the right. Something big glimpsed behind the sheets of rain. 'What are they?' Charlie calls from behind, the noise of the rain making her shout.

'Houses,' Cookey replies, making her blink and look again. Realising he's right and that the rain is so dense she can't see more than a few metres through it.

The shapes disappear. A hint of greenery. Thick bushes. The rain eases a touch, giving them glimpse of a wider open area as the Saxon rises over a slight bulge in the road and they navigate the bridge over the River Rother. The tide high. Only mere feet below, but they glimpse the waters that look calm and unmoving, save for the trillions of instantaneous strikes of raindrops hitting the surface.

At any other time it would be a beautiful place to stand and stare, and lose oneself to thoughts, but not now and not with that pressure inside.

By the time they reach the end of the short bridge, the rain is thick and once more so dense it blots the view on both sides, and all they can do is follow the Saxon as Maddox drives and follows the road ahead.

Structures on the left. Something colourful and striped. Awnings maybe. They pass under huge trees. The branches seemingly slouching, both from the intense wilting heat of the last month and now the heavy rainfall.

Surface water everywhere. The drains unable to cope. A month of bodies and litter being swept along by storms, and they're backed up so the roads flood with centimetres of water. Creating eddies and swirls.

They veer left. Passing a signpost directing them to the town centre and the harbour. The houses now much closer to the road. The same damage as seen everywhere else. Windows smashed in. Doors hanging off hinges. A body glimpsed in a doorway. The step already submerged under an inch of water, with more pouring into interior hallway.

On they go, with Charlie driving Jess as fast as she dares. Knowing what they've already been through. A day of non-stop battles behind them, and no sleep for nearly thirty-six hours. But the idea of Reginald being trapped or hurt, or even dying drives her on. She thinks to tell the Saxon to go on without them, but they don't have radios. All of their cheap, shit things melted in the fireballs at Gatwick. They don't have comms or a way to find each other.

'She's stopping!' Cookey calls, needing to feel like he's helping as the Saxon slows, then pulls over to the left.

Charlie speeds up. Seeing the larger commercial buildings loom out of the rain as the Saxon goes in close alongside them, with Howie leaning out the back doors.

'They're looking for supplies,' Cookey calls as they pass MOT service stations and garages within the old riverside buildings.

A flash of red. A long, glossy sign on the left. A construction supply store aimed for the timber industry, but with signs for DIY and groundwork, and general building materials. The Saxon slows, with Clarence dropping out of the passenger door before the vehicle stops. He strides to the door and with an explosion of power boots the centre section. Sending the entire door flying into the shop.

The rest bundle out. Dave and the dog going in first, followed by the others as the thunder rumbles closer, and Jess rears her head and turns in a circle.

'Why she doing that?' Cookey asks.

'Thunder makes her skittish,' Charlie says. 'Easy, Jess! Lean forward and pat her neck.'

Cookey does as told, leaning in to rub and pat Jess's hard, hot neck as the thunder rumbles on, deeper and lower, and louder.

A few seconds later, and the lads start running out

carrying armfuls of shovels and spades, and more hand tools.

Tappy sprints behind them but goes past the Saxon and past Charlie and Cookey on Jess.

'Where you going?' Cookey shouts.

'In there' she yells, seeing a commercial garage nearby with vans parked up outside.

Tappy heaves her axe at the glass pane in the reception door. Smashing it through before clambering inside. Thick dust on the ground. The air greasy and dry, and prompting a flurry of memories of her life spent in her father's workshop. Emotions spike inside. Bittersweet and filled with love. Then the bad images come. The ones from the night the outbreak started when she was attacked by her sister. They fell down the stairs together. Her mum was there. Her dad. Her brothers.

Tappy killed them all, using the kitchen knife that was stuck in her father's body. The knife she pulled from his chest.

Pain inside, and the panic threatens to well up and take over. She swallows and gasps, and shakes her head, with water and sweat spraying everywhere, and remembers Reginald trapped in the van. He could be hurt. He could be dead or dying.

She bursts to action and finds the key safe, and runs back to unlock the door and get outside, and starts clicking remotes, cursing foully at the new and shiny vans unlocking with indicators flashing.

'What's wrong with them?' Charlie asks as Cookey shrugs, not getting what Tappy is doing.

'That's the one,' Tappy says. Ditching the other keys back through the door and running to manually unlock the driver's door to a battered, old, faded red coloured Ford

Transit. The top few inches so bleached by the sun it looks pink.

'Why that one?' Cookey asks, but Charlie doesn't know why.

'Come on. Prove me right,' Tappy mutters, sliding the key in, pausing for the coil light to fade out. She pumps the pedal once and turns the key with the van firing up and chugging smoothly. 'Yes! You beauty! Royal Mail van!' she yells out the door to Charlie and Cookey. 'Older design. No modern electrics to fuck it up, and they were always serviced regularly. Honestly! These things are like tanks.'

She pulls out, with Charlie and Cookey, and the others coming out of the building supply shop, glancing over to the faded, old Royal Mail Delivery on the side. Something glorious about it, and very fitting that something so very British is being used to rescue Reginald.

They throw the tools in the red van. Hand tools. Chains. Ropes. Everyone rushing at a frantic pace.

'We clear?' Howie asks, getting the nod from Henry. 'Okay, load up! Split between the two vehicles.'

A few seconds. The vehicles start pulling out along the road as deep rolling claps of thunder sound directly overhead. Making Jess toss her head and skitter sideways while turning fast. The rain pelting down harder. Charlie works to keep Cookey in the saddle and Jess controlled at the same time as the thunder gets lower and louder, making Jess bolt the wrong way through a treeline and out onto a field.

Charlie shouts out, but her voice goes unheard over the rain and thunder as Jess gallops. Hating the noise that she can't see or know where it's coming from. Too deep. Too loud. Too everywhere all at the same time.

They pass vehicles parked on the grass nose to tail. Long and colourful. Structures looming in the rain. The striped awnings they saw before, but Jess spins and turns, frightened by the noise as she gains scent of something else through the rain.

Something wrong and bad.

She rears into the air. Charlie holds on from years of practise and adjusts her body to the flow.

Cookey doesn't and slides off when Jess turns and rears again, sending him flying into the wooden side of a brightly coloured hut.

He gasps for air as the thunder comes again, and the rain pelts down even harder. Blotting his view and losing all sight of Jess and Charlie.

'CHARLIE!' he shouts out, on his feet. He hears her voice but can't gain direction. He turns this way and that, trying to pinpoint where to go. Calling her name. Walking metres in each direction and losing all sense of where he is and which way to go.

Something moves nearby.

'CHARLIE!' he shouts and runs for it, but it's gone, and he clenches his hands, desperately frustrated at himself for falling off when they should be going for Reginald. A shout. Motion. 'Charlie!' he shouts and lunges to the figure moving ahead of him. The rain pelting his face. The bandage over his injured eye sliding down.

Something underfoot. He trips and goes down, and spots a thick power cable running across the grass, held down by a heavy, black, rubberised safety tube. But why is that here? He follows it along, thinking it'll take him to a building so he can shelter and wait for the rain to ease so he can see Charlie.

Something ahead. High and wide, with a striped awning.

A scuff. A snarl. He turns quickly, reaching for his axe that isn't there. No rifle either. Only his pistol and his knife.

Another scuff. Another snarl on the other side. He spins that way and backs up while drawing his sidearm, and walks into something slimy and wet. He spins around and feels his heart hammer at the striped material stretching up into the sky and out to the left and right. A certain shape to it. Blues and purples, and reds. The pattern and style that brings dread surging up inside.

Another snarl, followed by a sick, harsh cackle, and he spins back to see a once-painted face, now twisted in hunger, with a mop of orange hair on the head and black and white striped clothes, and big feet lunging at him. He screams and fires. Shooting it through the neck and turning to run, not stopping to see if it falls or dies.

Fear inside. Pure, awful fear from the thing that has always driven terror into his heart, and in his panic, he runs through the slit and into the big, striped circus tent.

6

Wet mud.

Reginald fingers it with his right hand. Rubbing the sand and chalk, and sediment mixture between his thumb and finger. Some of it bone dry. Some of it wet and sticky.

Knowledge forms instantly in his mind. Geology and the historical formation of the rocks in this area, and the layers of substrates formed over eons. He knows the chalk is a form of limestone made up from the minerals from the shells of marine life, which in turn means this area was once deep under water which, of course, would have changed as the continents drifted apart and the seas changed.

Reginald also knows that the famous white cliffs of Beachy Head and Seven Sisters are nearby. Both of them very high which indicates just how deep the waters in this region were hundreds of millions of years ago. But of course, it all turned to hot, wet swamps and went through ice ages and transitions that were varied and wild. Not unlike now, really. That said, the weather now is changing as a result of the near instant cessation of billions of people breathing and farting, and driving cars and buses, and boats, and flying planes, and using energy to heat their homes or to cool them.

It's not just the people either, but the by-products of the people, and Reginald strongly suspects that the sudden lack of management over the vast herds of cattle will also play a very significant part as cattle contribute enormously to the effects of greenhouse gases.

But then those cattle herds will still be there without slaughterhouses operating.

Ah, but dairy cows would have suffered if they hadn't been milked as their calves would have been taken away, which in turn will lead to infections and all sorts of nasties.

What a remarkably complex subject it is, and those thoughts all flow from one to the next within mere seconds of rubbing that wet mud between his fingers in the pitch dark.

Thinking soothes his mind. It brings calmness and rationality. Even when another chunk of wet mud plops down next to him. The chassis and frame groaning. The van shifting centimetres at a time. The panels buckling with thuds and bangs sounding muffled and far away.

More of the cliff coming down.

Burying him deeper.

Burying him alive.

What a way to go.

What a way for it to end.

He felt sure he'd get to the finish with Howie and get the Panacea out. He could visualise it happening.

But now this is happening, and it feels wrong.

Reginald snorts a dry laugh, thinking *to be honest, everything has felt wrong since Marcy gave him a kiss.*

'Will it hurt?' he asked her.

He even smiles into the darkness at the memory of it.

His face covered in blood from a gash on his head. The fingers on his left hand now gone but weirdly still hurting and even itchy. But then Reginald's knowledge means he is already aware of the phenomena of ghost limbs still having sensations long after amputation.

But yes. What a memory that is. So recent, but gosh, it feels such a long time ago now. And how scared he was back then too! Mind though, he was a timid man *before* the world fell. He stayed at home, living off the inheritance of his deceased parents in his small, neat flat. Reading books. Absorbing information. Learning. He used to take quizzes online to test himself. Reginald always scored high.

Then it happened, and the world came crashing down. He saw it unfold on the television before all the channels stopped broadcasting.

He stayed home. Eating sparsely and drinking water. Peeking out of the windows and seeing the shocking, awful, terrible carnage and violence. Reginald was smart and had seen them outside, sniffing around like dogs, and guessed they used scent to find prey. He put wet towels across the gap beneath his front door and kept spraying the inside with water to prevent smells leaking out.

Then they came for him, but it wasn't scent that brought them.

It was simply the fact that Marcy came into his building and calmly climbed the wooden stairs, with each step creaking as his heart thundered in his chest. His white shirt tucked in. His tie done up properly, because even while the world was ending, he still felt the need to be presented correctly.

Then it went silent, and he stood inside his flat staring at the front door for long seconds until the faint knocking made him yelp with fright.

'Open up,' Marcy said.

He didn't know she was called Marcy then. He could only hear her voice.

'I don't want to,' he told her.

'Please?'

'No. Just go away.'

'But I don't want to go away. I want to come inside.'

'You're not invited.'

'I'm not a vampire. It doesn't mean I can't come in unless I'm invited.'

'Well, you're not. So go away.'

'What's your name?'

'I'm not telling you.'

'Is it Reginald? You sound like a Reginald, and there was a post-box downstairs with the name Reginald on it. Is that you, Reggie?'

'It's Reginald! Not Reggie. I'm not an East End gangster.'

'So, you are Reginald then. Well. I'm Marcy.'

'Good for you, now please, go away.'

'I can't,' she whispered while tapping her fingernails lightly on the door. 'The bad things are near.'

'How do I know you're not one of the bad things?'

'Do the bad things talk, Reggie?'

'My name is Reginald, and just because I haven't seen them talk, doesn't mean they don't, or that they can't.'

He peeked through the spyhole at that point, but Marcy detected the motion and smiled broadly, and in so doing, he saw her eyes.

'You have red eyes,' he told her. 'The things have red eyes.'

'Oh, okay. Alright then. I am one of those things, and you are obviously a clever clogs. That's good. We need that.'

'Who needs that?'
'I do.'
'What for?'
'For my army.'
'What army?'
'I'm building an army.'
'Yes. We've established that. But whatever for?'

'For whatever I want. But I don't really know yet, because, dear Reginald, I'm the beauty, and now we need the brains.'

'You're not having my brains. They're perfectly fine in my head, thank you very much.'

'And in your head, they will stay.'

'I don't believe you.'

'Open the door, and I will prove it to you.'

'No! You'll bite me.'

'No, I won't. I shall kiss you instead, but only with your consent.'

'I don't consent!'

'But you will.'

'Why will I?'

'Because what choice do you have?'

'How is that consent if I don't have a choice?'

'Whatever. See. We need that level of thought. Right then. Open the door, and we'll get it done.'

'No!'

'Reggie! Open this door.'

'I will not!'

'I'll count to three.'

'I have a knife!'

'You don't have a knife. You don't sound the type to have a knife.'

'Well. I shall get one!'

'I'm going to open this door now, Reggie.'

'My name is Reginald, and do not open my door!'

'The key is in the lock, Reggie.'

'What key?'

'They key I found in your neighbours hallway that has a fob with the words *Reggie's spare keys* on it.'

'Blasted Mrs Smythe. I told her it was Reginald,' Reginald said, then yelped again as the door swung open.

'Wow. You didn't even put the bolts on,' Marcy said, giving him a look.

'I don't have bolts, but if you go away, I can fit some.'

She smiled that movie star smile. 'Or I could give you a little kiss. How about that?'

She stepped inside, thereby proving she was right when she said she wasn't a vampire and didn't need consent to come in. She looked incredible too. Radiant even. Long, thick, black hair and glowing skin, and a low-cut top showing off her cleavage, and Reginald could see more beautiful women behind her waiting silently.

'That's April,' Marcy said and pointed to the closest one. 'She was scared too, but I didn't bite her or any of them. April? Did I bite you?'

'No, Marcy,' April said, and Reginald wondered how Marcy and April could speak when the others that he'd seen were more like rabid animals.

'I'm unique,' Marcy said, guessing his thoughts.

'Or perhaps the thing inside you is,' Reginald said as she came closer, and he felt the terror welling up inside. But there was no way out. None at all, and there was no way Reginald could actually use a knife or any weapon for that matter. 'Will it hurt?' he asked.

'Not initially. You'll feel pain in your stomach, but it's quick, and then you'll feel no pain at all. Not ever again.'

'But I'll be mindless,' he said, fearing that more than anything else.

But Marcy didn't say anything. Instead, she pressed her lips to his. Reginald had never kissed a woman before, and he certainly never thought that his first kiss would be with someone as beautiful as Marcy. Not that it was a pleasant experience, given his state of abject terror.

She was right too because it didn't hurt initially. Then it did, and he dropped to the floor in agony. She knelt at his side and held his hand, and said it would be okay. He died looking up at her, and when he came back to life, she was still smiling, with April smiling behind her.

'Okay. See. Now get up and join the others,' Marcy said.

'To do what?' Reginald asked. 'I don't think it worked. Does that mean you'll go away now?'

'Oh,' Marcy said as she looked at him closely.

'Oh, what?' Reginald asked her.

'You can talk like me.'

'Well, yes, except, of course my English is better.'

'Right. Well. We'll let that one slide, you cheeky, little twat. Anyway! Welcome to my army.'

He got up and straightened his shirt and tie.

'You still haven't said what your army is for?'

'I don't really know myself,' she told him and started to walk off. He stayed behind, thinking that perhaps he was immune, but then, he felt something inside.

A strange compulsion, as it were. A *need* to be with Marcy, with an intense, deep sense of love for her. But not love in the romantic way.

'Come on then!' she called and looked at him like she knew he would follow, and to his amazement, he did and scurried after her, and in so doing, caught sight of his reflection, and his eyes now very red and bloodshot.

Marcy led him outside for the first time in a dozen days for Reginald to blink at the sun then at the many, many calm and controlled, and seemingly happy people Marcy controlled. Except, as Reginald would soon come to realise, they weren't actually people anymore. They had no freedom of thought but did only what Marcy told them or willed them to do.

'I think it's meant for something,' Marcy told him.

'What is?' Reginald asked.

'What I have. This disease, or whatever it is. Darren gave it to me then went after Howie, but he died.'

'Howie died?'

'No. Darren.'

'Oh.'

'Dave shot him.'

'And who is Dave?'

'He's with Howie! God, keep up. Anyway, I think Howie is connected. I'm sure we'll figure it out. But er, so these are all the zombies. Zombies, this is Reginald.'

'Hello, Reginald,' said the many zombies.

'Hello,' Reginald said then pressed his hand to his chest, then felt his own pulse. 'But we're not dead.'

'So?' Marcy asked, already losing interest in chatting.

'So then, we're not zombies. Zombies are dead.'

'What are we then?' she asked him.

Reginald didn't know what they were. 'How about *living challenged*,' he suggested as Marcy rolled her eyes and walked off, and like a puppy, Reginald ran after her.

Not that he had a choice back then. Seeing that whatever version she'd infected him with, compelled him to love, cherish, and adore her.

Which thankfully wore off as time went on.

But still. A bond does remain between them. As annoying and wholly blasted irritating as she is. And Marcy clearly loves Howie.

Whether that is because whatever strain Howie has *compels* them all to love him, or because of who Howie is, Reginald isn't entirely sure.

He sighs into the darkness as the van slides another foot, with crates of ammunition shifting and hitting his legs. He grunts and gets his legs free, then freezes at the sound of windscreen scraping clear of the fitting as the mud starts pouring in thick and fast.

7

THE TWO VEHICLES SET OFF FROM THE BUILDING supply store. The Saxon in the lead with Maddox driving. Tappy in the red van with Nick and Roy. Danny and Mo bundling in with her.

The rain pelting down, solid and sustained, and falling so hard they can't see more than a few metres. So they can't know that the same building supply store they entered backs onto a tributary of the River Brede, which in turn feeds into the wider and deeper River Rother, which feeds into the sea.

Nor could they know about the scores of vessels lined up along the River Brede or the slipways giving access to the full river.

They can't see it, so how *would* they know?

All they can do is face forward and keep following the signposts taking them towards the harbour on the A259, known locally as South Undercliff Road.

An ancient thoroughfare bordered with long terraces of old cottages butting up to the street leading to the ancient town of Rye. Houses with broken windows and broken doors, and broken bodies smashed through the broken picket fences.

But that's all they can see.

'We can't even radio him,' Howie says in the back of the Saxon, staring through the windscreen. 'He'll be okay though. I know he will be.'

Words given to keep their hope going, and he glances to the open back doors and that dense rain pelting the road behind them. The old Royal Mail van barely visible. 'Can anyone see Charlie and Cookey?'

Blowers leans fully out the back door, squinting at the rain lashing his face. Twisting to try and see left and right. 'CHARLIE? COOKEY?'

Tappy lifts a hand in the red van, cutting the others off as they talk. 'Did you hear that?'

'Hear what?' Nick asks, winding his window down to brave the rain and listen to someone shouting from ahead. 'YOU ALRIGHT?' he yells.

'I think I can hear Cookey,' Blowers says, pulling back into the Saxon.

'Alright. We can't be far now,' Howie says as they all turn to face forward, with the Saxon on a long, straight stretch. Terraces on the left. Bigger buildings on the right, with high trees between them bringing forth a feeling of being hemmed in and enclosed.

The building line on the right stops. A low wall after. The terraces end on the left. A feeling of reaching somewhere. A change in the road or a junction.

Maddox drives on. Leaning forward to try and see through the rain. Sweat and water pouring down his broad cheeks. Clarence the same. His stump still wrapped in gaffer tape. His clothes soaked to his body. Nerves inside all of them. Fear and worry.

The same in the red van behind them. Nick, Roy, and Tappy still talking about what boat to use as Mo's head seems to twitch as Danny looks at him.

'Shit! They's here!' Mo yells.

'Fuck,' Nick grunts and leans out the window to shout. 'INFECTED! THEY'RE HERE!'

Tappy hits the horn. Trying to get their attention.

Everyone in the Saxon snapping heads over to see the red van revving in close. Nick out the window yelling. Tappy on the horn. All of them waving.

'What the fuck,' Howie says.

'Pull over!' Paula calls.

Maddox turns back to face forward, with his foot coming off the accelerator as the front of the Saxon hits the outer ranks of the vast horde spilling across the road. 'FUCK!' he yells out, thinking he's hit a person and slamming the brakes on, with the van behind almost colliding.

All of them flying forward inside the vehicles from the sudden stop. Voices shouting as the wild roar of the infected goes up, and they swarm fast. Engulfing the front of the Saxon. Slamming faces into the thickened glass. Baring teeth, with crazed red eyes.

'Back up! Back up!' Howie yells as Blowers yells the same to Tappy, already selecting reverse and powering backwards as the infected hit the sides of the van.

Everything happening at once, with an infected getting her head through Nick's open window only for Meredith to lunge over Nick's lap and sink her teeth into the skull, and rag it side to side. Spraying Nick in hot, sticky, infected blood while Tappy reverses, and the Saxon does the same, with the engines whining noisily.

'Shit!' Tappy yells as a head comes through her open window. Danny reaches past her to try and heave it out.

Her feet momentarily coming off the pedals with enough loss of power for the Saxon to bridge the gap and slam into the front. Shunting them back, with Tappy yelling out and punching power to get away.

'We can't go back!' Howie yells. 'We need to get through them.'

'Howie, we need to retreat and replan,' Henry says.

'Fuck that,' Howie yells out, forcing his way to the back doors to leap onto the bonnet of the red van. He slips and slides, and almost falls off, but clings on, and leans over the side to kick the infected away from Tappy's door. 'Move over!'

'What the fuck are you doing?' Tappy yells at Howie trying to get through the window.

'Get out! Drive the Saxon. We need to get through.'

Tappy screws her face up. Not getting it for a full second before realising the play at hand. 'Got it! Nick, move!'

She scrambles over Nick trying to hold the wheel straight, with Howie climbing in, and Tappy going over the bonnet to leap into the Saxon. 'Mads! Let me drive.'

Mads goes left, with Tappy already piling over the seat into his place. The two vehicles still reversing at speed. Fishtailing and hitting walls, and smashing through fences.

'We need to go back!' Henry orders, waving at Howie to retreat.

'Negative, Major. The boss said to go through,' Tappy says, slamming her foot on the brake, with the red van shooting away before Howie slams his foot down to bring it to stop. The two of them gasping for air. Selecting first gear. Revving the engine. Gripping the steering wheel.

'Fuck me! HOLD ON!' Blowers shouts, gripping a

handrail before sending a foot into the face of an infected lunging in through the back doors.

Power applied. Engines roaring. The Saxon and the van move off as one. Building power, with Howie getting in nose to tail to the Saxon, knowing he has to ride her wake to get through.

'BRACE!' Tappy yells as everyone finds something to grip, and she slams into the horde, punching more power with the engine driving on, and that hard front end slamming them aside, with the big wheels crunching human forms. Snapping bones and making insides and brains pop out.

Noise and carnage. Tappy snarling. Howie the same. Keeping the van pressed to the Saxon. Sparks flying from the physical contact.

'There's a lot of them!' Clarence shouts from the front as they spill out from the narrow road to see a junction leading off and buildings on South Undercliff Road butting up to the edge of the River Brede. The tide so high the waters are spilling over the grass verge, creating a shallow lake across the road.

Hundreds of infected, thick across the road and stretched off ahead, surrounding the buildings facing the river. Old warehouses turned into pubs. 'Survivors,' Clarence calls. Knowing that the infected must have been trying to get inside those buildings to some survivors inside.

'SURVIVORS INSIDE AHEAD!' Blowers yells out the back to Howie.

Howie nods once. Grim-faced and sensing the horde is far bigger than they expected to see in such a small place.

'What's the plan?' Tappy shouts from the front.

'We're winging it,' Paula replies, shooting a frantic look

back to Howie as the Saxon rocks and bounces from the impacts of the infected and going over the mangled bodies.

'Where's the harbour?' Howie asks.

'I don't know, but the river is right there,' Nick says, trying to see higher out the window. 'I can't see anything. Fuck it.'

'What are you doing?' Howie yells as Nick pivots and squeezes through the open window to mount the bonnet, slipping and sliding, and falling into the back of the Saxon and gets up through the hole to get on the roof to view the river.

'Clever fucker,' Howie says.

'It goes round!' Nick shouts down the hole.

They pass the buildings on the right. Seeing faces in the high upper windows, and the lower doors and windows barred and barricade. The horde thick and plentiful, with hundreds more than Howie first thought, and that hope seems to dwindle. They can't see the signposts or where the harbour is, and in this mess, they can't even tell what direction to take. They might have to do Henry's suggestion and retreat to come up with a plan B.

But Nick spots something through the squall of rain. The flash of an outline and nothing more. A silhouette even. A shape of something on the river. But a distinctive shape. 'TUG!'

'TUG WHAT?' Howie yells back.

'He wants something tugged,' Frank tells the others in the Saxon.

'Not tugged. Tug!' Carmen shouts. 'TUG *BOAT!*'

'Oh, that'll do it,' Roy says, reading her lips.

'Tell them to do a loop round. DO A LOOP!' Howie mouths at Paula, circling a hand around the buildings.

'Do a loop, Tappy!' Paula relays, nodding back at Howie.

'On it!' Tappy says, turning the wheel to navigate the end of the building line and stay on the circular road running around it back to where they came in.

'How the hell are we getting to that tug?' Paula asks and holds her hands up to Howie, asking him silently how they can do this.

'We need to retreat and come in from the other side,' Henry shouts to Howie while motioning them to go back.

'NO TIME!' Howie shouts. Knowing that if by some miracle Reginald is still alive, then he won't have long before either the air runs out or the van is crushed by the cliff and buried forever.

And that can't happen.

They need Reginald.

They need Reginald more than they need Howie. The team has Henry now, but nobody else can do what Reginald does. Not even Charlie.

In which case there really is no question then, and in that second Paula stares out through the back of the Saxon, holding Howie's eyes. Sensing the same. Thinking the same. Knowing what has to happen. She nods at Howie. He nods back.

Decision made.

Go for the tug, Howie mouths. *Me and Dave will draw them off.*

A quick thumbs up from Paula. 'Tappy! Go for the tug. Nick! Guide us in. We're going for the tug…'

A pop, pop, pop in the air.

Gunfire in the distance, coming from behind.

Paula cuts off. Lunging to the back to stare out. 'Where's Charlie and Cookey?'

'Fuck!' Howie gasps. Twisting to try and see them.

Pop, pop, pop.

Gunfire again.

'We've fucking lost them!' Paula says, her mind running fast. Howie nodding at her. Urging her to give the orders that he can't give because he's in the other van. 'Danny! Mo!' she yells, getting eye-contact from them both in the red van while she uses her hands to signal. 'You two. Go back to Charlie and Cookey. RUN FAST!'

Mo and Danny nod. Getting the play. Knowing they can outrun any horde.

'Henry,' Paula says, turning back to the others. 'You take everyone to the tug and get to Nick. I'll work with Howie and Dave to draw them away. All of you, listen in! Get to Reginald. Do not stop. Do not come back for us. Reginald is the priority. Am I clear?'

'You get that?' Howie calls to the others in the red van. 'Second we stop, Danny and Mo, you go back to find Charlie and Cookey. 'READY!' he yells at Paula.

They start the turn back along the front of the buildings, with Nick straining to see through the rain. 'LEFT A BIT, TAPPY!'

'Left a bit,' Frank relays as Tappy eases the wheel to steer left. Seeing only infected and rain ahead.

'LEFT AGAIN!'

'Left again!'

'NOW STRAIGHT!'

'Straight!'

'ALMOST!'

'Almost.'

'STOP, STOP, STOP!'

'Stop, stop, stop!'

Tappy brakes.

Howie brakes.

Everyone moves.

Dave out of the Saxon, leaping clear with his knives drawn to gracefully swipe left and right, slitting throats to buy space for Danny and Mo to get out of the van's sliding door. The two lads moving low and fast. Building speed while dodging, and weaving to get through the horde.

Roy out the front passenger door and reaching in to start grabbing the tools from the red van while Dave protects his back. Howie joins him, catching the axe thrown by Paula and swiping out to take one down before moving out to clear space. Paula on Dave's other side. Hacking into them with her machete. Marcy with them. Choosing to stay with them rather than go with the others.

Pure chaos ensues as Howie, Dave, Paula, and Marcy shout and holler, and attack the horde to lure them off to the side while the others grab the tools, with Nick already off the Saxon and running towards the shape of the tug looming out of the rain. A sweeping bow line with thick sides protected by old tyres roped together and powerful engines at the back. The marine version of the Saxon.

He vaults the side and lands hard on the wet metal deck, then he's up, slipping and sliding to the wheelhouse. Shooting a window out with his pistol before reaching in to open the door from the inside.

Then he's in and dripping water while heaving for air and scanning the controls. Unable to read any of the words. But in his mind the schematics of the boat glow clear, turning over on end as he determines the flow of power and fuel lines. The steerage. The electrics and mechanical layout of all the moving parts needed to make this thing operate. His lips moving. His eyes seeing it all. His fingers dancing over the levers and controls. The infection enhancing his own natural abilities.

'NICK!' Roy shouts as the tools get thrown into the back of the tug with a clang.

'It's coming, it's coming,' Nick murmurs. Learning how to make it work as quickly as Reginald reads complex text in a book.

'NICK!' Clarence bellows. 'We'll get overrun!'

'Best hurry up then,' Nick mutters and flicks a switch to activate the flow

of fuel then another to make sure the fuel pumps are working. Then another to switch the power on before he thumbs a switch to the sound of a clunk. *Hmmm. That wasn't right.*

'NICK!' come the many shouting voices.

'Ah,' Nick says, rolling his eyes at seeing the words **on / off** on the toggle over the engine ignition switch. He flicks it to **on** and tries again, and the powerful engines thrum to life. 'Fuck yes!'

'GO ON, NICK!' Tappy's voice from somewhere makes him grin as he runs out to start throwing the mooring ropes off, but they're too taut from a month of high and low tides, dragging the tug this way and that.

'GET IN!' he yells and pulls his knife to cut through the rope at the front, with the boat starting to pull out into the river within a second, and the others leaping and falling over the sides. Henry, Carmen, and Frank. Blowers. Mads. Booker. Clarence and Bash in the rear. Bash using his long knife while Clarence swings a metal pole one handed to buy time for the others to get boarded. 'GET IN!' Nick shouts with his blade pressing the stern line as Bash and Clarence vault over the side, and the boat starts drifting out into the river. The infected trying to leap and getting stabbed and pushed into the river.

Nick runs back into the wheelhouse, with Henry grabbing the wheel and pushing the lever forward to apply power. Making the waters at the back of the boat froth from the propellers as the bow seems to lift from the momentum.

A last glance back at the shore. To the hundreds of infected turning away to follow a single shouted voice drifting through the rain.

'I. AM. DAVE!'

8

Cookey stumbles into a deafening silence.

Except it's not silent. It just seems that way from being out of the hard rain pelting his head and ears. Now it just hits the top and sides of the tented structure, painted in bright lurid stripes. Reds. Purples. Blues.

The dread spikes inside. An awful, gripping feeling of absolute terror as he spins around in a circle. His body soaked. His torn and shredded clothes clinging to his body. His blond hair plastered to his scalp. The filthy wet bandage sagging down. His single blue eye now not twinkling or full of mirth, but instead wide with crushing, debilitating fear.

This happened before.

The day when it was foggy. They ran and ran for miles, and ended up in a circus. Cookey froze up then too, but he had the others to get him out.

Now there's nobody.

He's alone and trapped in the worst place he could ever be trapped in, surrounded by cackling evil laughs and ragged hisses, and deep, long snarls coming from all sides.

He twists and turns. Gasping and whimpering. Wishing Charlie was here. Or Jess, but Charlie can't see the tent in the pouring rain, and in her own sense of horror, she realises the circus ground is full of infected. All of them snarling and lunging in as she stays on Jess, firing her pistol to give Cookey a sound to aim for while he stands alone inside the big top. Not hearing the gunshots. His mind unable to function because of the terror inside.

His pistol in his hand that he aims at the snarls and cackles. Not knowing where they're coming from, and that whimper gets worse when he realises with a deeper sense of terror and humiliation that he's pissing himself in fear.

Just like when he was a child.

When the irrational fear started.

Only it wasn't an irrational fear at all.

It was a fear created by his brain carving a neural pathway, designed to be used in times of pure survival to get him away from danger.

The danger posed by predators.

A predator of a different sort.

He was so young. Four, maybe five. He didn't like clowns. He got upset at the circus. His mum called him a coward and said he needed to get over it. But to Cookey they were weird and sinister, and they didn't look funny or sweet at all.

His mum made one of her drinking buddies dress as a clown with make-up and big feet, and a wig of thick, brightly coloured hair. Cookey was forced onto a chair in the kitchen as the clown stalked towards him. Cackling and jumping around. Cookey pissed himself in fear then as he does now.

His mother told her friend to keep doing it and said Cookey needed to be saturated with his fear to get over it.

She went out to the pub.

She left Cookey alone with the clown.

Cookey cried and wept, and the man inside the clown costume finally stopped. He said he was sorry. He spoke kindly.

The man noticed Cookey had wet himself.

He took Cookey to the bathroom.

The man touched Cookey. Then he touched himself. He pinned Cookey against a wall and said if Cookey ever told anyone what they did, he'd come back and eat him.

That memory seared into Cookey's mind.

That painted face, with the hands on his little neck. The big, red, fake smile. The big, black and white panda eyes.

Now he pisses himself with fear again because the neural pathway is still there and driving the chemical reactions the same as when he was tiny and vulnerable.

The need to run and get away while simultaneously rooting him to the spot with such fear that he can't form the thought to do anything other than react to the noises. Spinning and twisting, then crying out when he turns to see a clown shuffling slowly into the tent. The big, red smile all worn and bloodied. The skin sallow and covered in paint and gore. The wig gone. A bald head underneath, covered in bites and cuts that writhe with maggots. Black and white clown clothes, and only one oversized boot.

Another scuff to the side.

Cookey twists to see another clown lurching through the slits in the big circus tent. Orange hair. Bloodied, red cheeks. His lower lip bitten away, showing filthy, rancid teeth drooling with saliva. The same black and white clothes. The same big feet.

Cookey tries to lift and aim his pistol. His hand trembling so much the shot would miss by a mile. Motion on the right. He lurches around and cries out again at a woman clown coming in. A huge, fat belly, with one heavy, sagging breast hanging free of her torn clothes. Half of her face torn off, with her eyeball bouncing on a thread of tendon as she snarls and hisses.

Another scuff from behind.

A clown with dwarfism.

Wild hair, and a face full of fury. His right arm just a stump of scabbed blood. Another clown with dwarfism joins the first. Then another and another.

Cookey backs away and spins to see more fat and skinny clowns pushing through the tent sides. Fat clowns. Skinny clowns. Tall and short clowns.

They're not just clowns either but workers, and circus performers. Not that Cookey sees anything but clowns. All of them in painted faces and curly wigs, and big feet. All of them coming forward at the same time towards Cookey in the middle of the tent.

Hissing and snarling.

Cackling and growling.

Coming for him.

Coming to eat him.

9

They'll come for him.

Reginald knows that.

He has worth to them. Especially to Howie. Howie knows Reginald is the key to leading them to the people that started it, so Howie can have the revenge he so desperately needs.

But Reginald also knows his worth is more than any transactional arrangement between them.

That's how it started, of course, with Reginald using his intelligence to aid Howie's endeavours, and in turn, day by day, they became closer, until Reginald was no longer the odd, little man that came with Marcy, but as much a member of the pack as any of them.

So, yes.

Reginald knows they will come for him.

What Reginald cannot determine, however, is *if* they are *able* to come for him. And *if* they are able to find the *right* means and method, and then there is also a big *if* about whether they can actually find his position, given that there was a very large section of the cliff falling down. Which most likely covered the whole of the van *and* the SUV, and the horse trailer.

Ah, but at least Jess got clear.

That's good.

Charlie has already lost Blinky. Losing Jess would crush her. He grimaces at the feeling inside when he thinks about never seeing Charlie again. But then he feels that way when he thinks about not seeing any of them again. Even Marcy to some small degree. Certainly Paula and Roy who can be very pleasant company sometimes.

Reginald smiles at the thought of Danny and Mo and wishes he'd got to know them better, but he also knows Carmen will keep an eye on the two lads. She's certainly taken them under her wing. She's a very nice person too. Always very polite and friendly to Reginald. Making him herbal teas and checking on him.

'Everything okay?' she would ask between the battles.

'Yes! Fine. Thank you,' he'd tell her.

'Another tea?'

'Oh gosh, no. I am not equipped with a large bladder. And do forgive me sharing that knowledge which I am sure you did not want to hear.'

Carmen laughed. 'You can tell me anything you want, Reginald.'

He liked being called Reginald. Nobody ever called him Reginald now. Only Reggie. Which he used to despise, but truth be told, he's become rather fond of it.

He's even become fond of the incessant humour between the lads and will often chuckle at the raucous banter and smile at the jokes about penises and such like, although not when they are watching of course. He does like to maintain an appropriate air of intellectualism.

But well, now.

There you go.

His journey is coming to an end.

At least he gave instructions to Lilly.

"If we fail, you must reduce the numbers before you release the panacea. Releasing the panacea too soon will not work. Cull the infected first, so they cannot overrun the survivors."

Reginald told that to Lilly *before* she pulled guns on Henry and made him tell her where the Panacea was. Which Reginald was very disappointed in, but then Lilly is young, and the young are always foolish.

Mind you. It's not just the young that are foolish. Marcy is certainly foolish a lot of the time.

'Girls, I think Reggie needs a kiss,' Marcy bursts out laughing as the gorgeous group led by April move towards Reginald, all of them smiling and showing him their charm.

'Marcy, you're stopping me from running away,' Reginald told her. 'This is not fair... Let me run away... Oh my, yes, thank you, hello, very nice to meet you. Shall we just shake hands instead? No... Oh, right... Oh, another one... Yes, well, this is very pleasant, and yes, hello to you too. Oh, another kiss... Marcy! This is intolerable... Yes, my dear, I am very pleased to meet you. Really there is no need to keep kissing me...'

Reginald grunts at the memory of Marcy making her attractive hosts kiss and fawn over Reginald back when they first met while at the same time as exerting her will to stop him running away.

Which, when thought back, was clearly very wrong, but still, it is quite comical when he thinks back now, and he snorts again when he remembers the time they were in the sex shop.

'Good god, have you seen the size of these...monstrosities?' Reginald asks in horror holding a long, thick, pink coloured dildo up as though captivated at the absurd size of the object. 'Do women actually use these things? I mean the size of it... Doesn't it cause horrendous injury? Have you ever...' his voice drops off as a look of realisation steals across his face, a sudden awareness of the question he was about to ask.

'Reginald! Were you about to ask me if I ever used a giant dildo?'

Marcy went on about that for a very long time. Although it really wasn't long ago at all. It just feels that way because their perception of time has changed. Which is because their lives are not dictated by the concept of measured time anymore.

Another plop of wet mud hits his face, and he leans to the side to sluice it free, wincing at the pain in his left hand coming from the stumps of his severed fingers.

Mud around his legs. He tries to get higher to keep clear of it. Sinking back in and groping out to use his desk first as a lever to grip on and then as a platform to stand on as the mud inside the van rises higher.

He gropes above him, feeling the doorway to the cabin

and knowing he has only a few feet left before he's swallowed alive.

At least he was able to wrap Nick's drone in some plastic. He found a roll of bin liners and busied himself, with only one fully functioning hand and in the dark, tearing them apart to secure around the drone.

Another flurry of mud pours past and on him, and he fights to get his feet free and pushes through the door, and gropes out to feel the steering wheel and the hilt of Roy's sword.

Then he reaches up and grimaces at the feel of the mud where the windscreen was. Wet, cloying mud mixed with chalk and earth. Pebbles and stones too. Which make it impossible to dig through with bare hands. He thinks about using Roy's sword to hack it away, but it won't do any good.

This is it then.

He's counting down the minutes as the mud pours in and rises towards the wall of mud that will bury him alive.

10

'WE NEED THEM AFTER US!' HOWIE SHOUTS AS THEY dance back but see only a small part of the horde coming after them with many more aiming for the others carrying the tools to throw into the tug. 'Fuck's sake!' he shouts and runs in deep to swing his axe in fury. Slicing through necks and shoulders. Arms and legs. Hollering and shouting to draw attention. Paula, Marcy, and Dave do the same. Attacking with wild abandon. Blood spattering their faces as the hard rain pelts down. But it's not enough.

'NICK!' Clarence's voice as he fights next to Bashir while the others bundle into the tug. 'WE'LL GET OVERRUN!'

'You go!' Tappy yells, bursting away from Clarence as she dodges and weaves through the horde to get back to the Saxon, and a second later, they all hear the deep throaty roar of the tug's engines. 'GO ON, NICK! Tappy yells and stabs an infected man through the neck, and flings him away from the driver's door, and bundles inside, then turns to kick another one away, so she can slam the door, expecting the dog to come to her aid, but then figuring Meredith must have gone with Nick or stayed with Howie.

Then the shout goes up.

The big one, with Dave's voice booming out from somewhere nearby. **'I AM DAVE!'**

'Get the fuck off!' Tappy snarls and boots the infected attacking her through the door away, then gasps at the sight of the horde turning as one to go after Dave. A gap formed with a fleeting glimpse to the tug floating away from the side of the river, pulled by the tide before the water at the back froths and the engines bite to drive it away.

Tappy twists fast, slamming the door and revving the Saxon's engine as if in reply and pulls out while turning hard to slam a few infected down. Doing what she can to ease the pressure on the boss and the others.

'That fucking worked!' Howie cries out as the horde all turn as one and start their charge. 'Shit, shit, shit... RUN!'

Paula and Marcy don't need telling twice, and the four slip on the wet road as they start gaining traction to run up The Strand behind The Ship Inn, with the faces of the survivors staring down from the windows in terror and awe at four people being chased by hundreds of infected.

A wide junction ahead. An ancient crossroads where five lanes meet, bordered by old cottages and old inns.

A narrow road to the hard right. Howie aims for it. Knowing it will impede the size of the horde by forcing their width down. They sprint into the junction, with their feet slipping on the soaking wet cobblestones of Mermaid Street.

'Shit!' Paula snaps, going down, with Marcy pulling her up while Dave turns and fires his pistol into the first infected coming after them. Getting headshots with each bullet fired, but the press comes too much, and they soon start running again, with surface water cascading down the street towards them.

A roar behind them. The Saxon slams past the junction, taking down a swathe of infected as it goes by, but more fill the spaces and screech with wild hunger as Howie leads them on. Running up the narrow lane. Tudor houses on the left and right. Old wooden doors and old wooden windows smashed and broken.

Henry at the helm in the tug. Nick and Carmen at the prow, straining to see through the rain lashing their faces as they navigate the River Brede. The sides of the tug hitting other vessels floating free from a month of rising and falling tides and wild storms snapping mooring ropes.

'Down!' Carmen yells, pulling Nick below the lip as the tug smashes through a beautiful, slender yacht, with masts and sails coming down over them. The others rush over to help heave it overboard as Henry fights to see the way ahead. Hitting the banks and slewing left to right.

It takes too long, and Henry starts to think they've gone the wrong way. Nick feels it too. Sharing a look of intense worry with Roy.

'Look!' Carmen calls, straining to see as they all peer through the falling rain to see the banks on either side end as the Brede joins the much wider River Rother. 'Go right!' Carmen shouts.

'My right or yours?' Henry calls.

'Starboard, Major!' Blowers relays.

'Thank you, Marine,' Henry says with a nod as he turns the wheel and pushes the vessel out onto the cleaner waters, and punches the power with the boat surging on towards the sea.

Behind them on the land, Danny and Mo run with everything they have back along South Undercliff Road. Neither talking to save breath, and so they can listen as they search for Charlie and Cookey.

Charlie turns on Jess. Way ahead of Danny and Mo on the large green at the edge of town. Cursing at it not just being a circus but a fairground too with rides and kiosk-trucks, and structures everywhere. She rides on. Shouting for Cookey, without having an axe or machete to use to keep the infected away. All she can do is let Jess twist and turn, and use her size and agility to keep them clear, but that means she can't stay still and listen. 'COOKEY!' She screams his name over and over as Jess rears and drops hard to slam an infected down, then back kicks another one so hard it flies back metres and hits something with the dong of a bell. Charlie twists in the saddle. Recognising the sound. 'Yes!' she gasps on seeing it and slides off to grab the big, heavy mallet used by men showing off to their dates to strike the target and ring the bell to win a cuddly toy, mass produced by children locked in factories.

Back to Jess, and she mounts fast, with her feet finding the stirrups, and the horse turning as she swings the mallet over and slams it down into a skull that bursts apart with a spray of pink. 'Good god, that's brutal!' she says in awe of the heavy, wooden hammer with two thick bands of iron around the ends. Now all she needs to do is find Cookey, but she still can't see through the rain.

Cookey still can't hear Charlie or anything else for that matter. Only the blood roaring past his ears while he feels only the mind-numbing terror of being surrounded by clowns on all sides.

All of them drawing closer and closer. Rotten wigs and faded, painted faces. Torn lips and filthy teeth. Hissing. Snarling. One cackles with a memory of the laugh he used to use in this very tent, and in the centre, Cookey gibbers with fright. Rendered still and unable to do anything other than tremble from head to toe.

Reginald feels that same primeval sense of fear threatening to overwhelm him with fight or flight chemicals releasing into his body. Except he cannot fight, and he certainly cannot give flight. There is nowhere to go, and he slowly gets closer and closer to that wall of wet, crumbling earth, threatening to break apart and fall inside.

He angles to lie across the rising mud beneath him. Buying a few moments more of life while knowing deep down it won't do any good. He hasn't heard them. They are not coming.

They *are* coming, but the River Rother is long and twists, and turns, and Henry doesn't dare punch maximum power for fear of beaching the vessel. He can't see the sides or where the water shallows out.

'We think. We plan. We succeed,' he mutters, suppressing the urge to go faster.

Danny and Mo breathe hard, with their arms pumping, and the rain splashing their faces. Making it hard to see, but they snatch a view of a long, glossy, red sign ahead for the timber place they raided and share a glance. Knowing this must be where they got separated.

The top of Mermaid Street in the village of Rye. The Mermaid Inn off to one side, now burnt and blackened from a raging fire that tore through on the first night. Caused by a selfish, greedy, old man setting fire to the place so he could escape the infected while knowing people were trapped upstairs.

Not that Howie and the others pay it a second glance as they run past. Gasping for air with the rain lashing their faces.

'My fucking hair,' Marcy says. Her hair band broken, and the spares worn on her wrists lost in the Battle for Gatwick. Paula the same. The wet strands getting loose and flapping down over her cheeks and eyes.

She risks a look back and double takes at a low wall topped with coils of razor wire, and guesses it must lead to the compound at the rear of a bank on the main road.

'Howie, axe!' she shouts, running over as Howie turns and follows her, passing the axe as Paula grunts and chops over her head at the wooden struts holding the coiled wire in place. She runs on, chopping the next one, with Dave drawing his sidearm and changing magazine to fire into the horde.

'We have to go!' Marcy yells.

'Last one,' Paula says and strikes the last strut before using the axe head to snag the coiled wire as she pulls back with a hard yank. 'Help me!'

Howie rushes in, with them both yanking and tugging the razor wire down and across the street.

'Go, go, go!' Marcy yells, firing her own pistol at the horde. They all fall back. Howie and Paula slipping and helping each other up, while casting glimpses back to the front line of the horde slamming into the coiled wire. Slicing into skin and flesh, but more importantly, tangling their feet and making them fall which makes the ones behind trip and snag and, compress. 'Nice!' Marcy says, high-fiving Paula.

But it's not enough. The infection doesn't care about its own hosts. Not with this horde anyway. All they want is to rake and bite, and attack. That's the single driving force within them, and so Paula and the others turn to flee. Sprinting out of Mermaid Street and taking a right along a wider road as the horde spill free of the narrow lane and roar as they speed up and start closing the gap.

They follow the flow of the road to the left and burst out into a church garden. Splashing through nearly a foot of water caused by the incessant rain and the hard ground being unable to soak it up. On they go. Gasping and falling to splash and scramble up. Round the side of the church. Bodies in the entranceway. A once barricaded door smashed open and smeared with blood.

Out onto another street. The same styles of houses on

the left and right. Suburbia in all its rotten glory. BMWs. Mercedes. Range Rovers on driveways. If they had time, they'd stop and search for keys, but there isn't time to do anything but run. No rifles. One axe. Two machetes, and Dave with a pistol and a knife against several hundred raging infected, and that's *after* the day before the Battle for Gatwick. No sleep. Not enough food, and despite the rain, they haven't taken fluids on since they left the big airport to return to their own, now broken and ruined, smaller airfield, and from all of those things, the sense of hopelessness starts to hit. That of all the places it will be here, in the tiny town of Rye where old men committed murder to stay alive, that will see them fail and die.

That same feeling inside of Cookey. That same awful, gut-wrenching, deep feeling of utter despair mingled with terror gripping his heart. Robbing his mind of the ability to think. Freezing his body to the spot as the clowns gain closer and closer. Close enough to smell. Close enough to feel the heat coming from them. Close enough to bring back the memories of the clown that pinned him to the wall in the bathroom when he was tiny. He smelt the tobacco and booze on the man's breath and felt the heat coming from him then.

The same now.
The same then.
The same Cookey.
Trapped.
Tiny.
Defenceless.

Charlie outside, slamming the mallet into heads as the infected swarm at her. She knocks them down and bursts on another few metres. Searching in vain. The water pouring from the sky, blotting her view. The sense of hopeless despair rising inside as more and more infected surge out of the squalling greyness. Driven only to rake and bite, and attack.

Danny and Mo running with everything they have. Hitting the edge of the field as they spot branches, freshly broken, and a muddy horse print on the bank. They vault and slide, gasping in the rain, heaving for air, and once more set off while knowing the chances of finding anyone in this weather is near on impossible.

The same in the tug as they finally reach the end of the river, and Henry pushes the speed to full to make the engines roar as the froth behind them becomes a thick, churned wake in the otherwise still water of the open sea. The rain pelting harder than before. Drenching them all as they switch from staring ahead to looking left at the coastline. Searching through the water coming down for signs of cliff falls.

A shunt on the portside makes Henry veer starboard as he spots the browner hue in the sea and remembers Camber Sands. The big sandbank famous for the nice beaches. They can't risk beaching here, so he punches out into the open sea and on, until that brown hue fades and becomes the deep green. Only then does he take the vessel back in as close as he dares to the shore. Passing a holiday park and houses. All of them the same as everywhere else. Broken and burnt. Ruined and rotten, and that despair rises in all of them. That everything is taking too long.

They all feel it.

That sense of hopeless despair, but perhaps none so acute as in Reginald as he gasps in the confined space. Trapped on top of the gloopy layer of wet mud rising beneath him.

His ruined left hand held close to his body. His right hand clawing at the wall of mud and stones. Gouging tiny holes out that do nothing more than pour sediment and filth into his eyes.

He whimpers in fear when his body presses into the wall of mud. His legs starting to sink with nowhere else to go. The water pouring into the van, making the mud beneath him more liquid and less viscous.

Fear spikes, with images of his life flashing through his mind. Except there are very few images of his life before now. Before meeting Marcy. Before the brave, new world.

His flat. His collection of books. The shop he used for groceries. That's it. Nothing more, and there's no real feeling attached to those images and memories either. It was just a life he once had. A life *before* his life started for real.

This life.

His life with Howie and Paula, with Clarence, and Roy, and all the others. Real friends. More than friends. Family. And with them he transitioned from a nobody into a real somebody, leading the fight back. My god, they fought back, and he grins with fury at what they did as his body sinks, and the mud rises over his chest. They did that. They fought back and refused to be cowed, and they got up after each filthy, dirty, nasty brawl to do it again. And again. And again.

Like now, with Charlie swinging her mallet with wild fury at being prevented from reaching Cookey.

Like now, with Danny and Mo hitting the edge of the field used for the fair and circus and drawing blades as the infected turn and charge at them.

Like now, as Howie bursts out onto Rye High Street, with the horde screeching behind.

'Dave, grenade!' Paula shouts. Knowing Dave always has one hidden. Dave shoots her a look. Not wanting to use it. 'Fuck's sake, Dave! Now!'

He hands it over as Paula turns towards scaffolding erected high and wide across several listed buildings. 'Buy me time!'

'Fuck!' Howie grunts and runs into the horde to chop them down. Dave at his side. As graceful as ever. Dancing his dance. Slicing out left and right as they fall with cut arteries. But the press is fast and hard, driving them back, with an infected female grabbing Marcy's hair in a clawed hand.

Marcy lashes out with the machete, cutting the woman's stomach open. The entrails pour out, but the beast clings on and drives forward, smashing Marcy through a window of a shop as Marcy chops hard to sever the arm and throw the limb at another one coming at her.

She heaves herself up, feeling something soft in her grip from inside the shop. A beret snatched from a display. She sweeps her hair back and tugs it on before snarling and running back to chop and kill, and fight in another filthy, dirty, nasty brawl. Getting knocked down but getting back up. Refusing to die. Refusing to be cowed.

Cookey in the tent. The panic so high he's close to hyperventilating. The fear has won. The terror has succeeded. His day is lost. He can't fight anymore. He can't do a thing. A hand reaches out and grabs his neck. His legs give way. The beast drives him down, and that once painted face and curly orange hair, and red bloodshot eyes loom close to the tiny child, ready to devour him, ready to kill him.

This is it for Reginald too. The last few seconds of life, and that rush of power he felt from the memories of them fighting fade away, leaving him alone and scared, and about to die, trapped in the darkness. Suffocating. Drowning. Being crushed as the mud rises, and he presses into that wall of mud.

His voice whimpers, and his eyes clamp shut as the mud rises over his chin. His face against the wall.

This is it.

This is his time to die.

Cookey the same.

His eyes clamp shut as he sinks onto his back, and the clowns claw at his body, with their mouths readying to rake and bite, and attack. Saliva drips onto his skin, and he tenses every part of his body. Knowing this is it.

This is his time to die.

Both seeing the images of their lives flashing behind their eyes. Cookey seeing Blowers and Nick, and how his life changed at Salisbury. Mr Howie. Dave. Paula. Reggie. Blinky. Jamie. Curtis. Tucker. Faces and feelings. Then, Charlie. Oh, Charlie! Her brown eyes. Her shaved head. Despair and loss inside. Regret too. Regret that he never told her how he feels.

Reginald the same. Full of fear and regret.

Both of them full of turmoil before their brains release the final chemical of life.

The chemical that brings instant, soothing calm as they transition from life into death, and as one, at the same time, they both feel sudden and deep inner peace steal over them and pull them away from the abject terror.

A deep inner peace that tells them they can let go now.

That they've done enough.

That they have *given* enough.

They give thanks for the time they had, and they give thanks for the honour of knowing the others as Reginald sinks fully into the mud, and the hands around Cookey's neck tighten and draw blood, and the teeth find his arms and legs. His shoulders and stomach.

A sense of falling in both of their minds.

Falling into darkness.

Into a void.

The tugboat powering on.

Carmen staring at the coast with wide eyes. Her hands gripping the side, with her knuckles turning white.

Dave killing everything in his path, but even he can't kill fast enough.

The end.

The end.

The end is coming, and nothing will ever be the same again as Charlie feels that pressure inside and screams so loud it gives direction to Danny and Mo who run to give aid as Jess rears, and the rain falls hard, while Cookey and Reginald fall and fall, and fall into the darkness of the void.

Both about to die.

Both ready to die.

But in the blink of an eye. In the beat of a heart. Everything can change.

Paula pulls the pin in the grenade and drops it, before screaming at the other three as they sprint across the road and dive through the window broken by Marcy. A second later the grenade detonates and blows the support struts of the scaffolding out, and the whole lot collapses down onto the horde below, with Paula's eyes gleaming in victory.

'KILL THEM!' Howie roars, and those four charge into the dust and chaos as the Saxon slams into the back of the horde.

Tappy shouting out as she changes gear and pulls the vehicle back, and tears a chunk from the corner of an ancient house with a jarring jolt that knocks her MP3 player, with the random selection triggered, and a second later the jaunty intro starts to *The Ketchup Song*. The device still connected to the loudspeakers, with the music blasting out to fill the streets of Rye, and in the blink of an eye, and the beat of a heart, everything can change.

'There!' Carmen yells on the tugboat. Every head snatches over to the long section of coast, now fallen down, but with one contrasting object poking out. The broken and mangled white side of the horse box.

The blink of an eye.

The beat of a heart.

A will exerted through all of them from one mind that never falters.

Not once.

Not ever.

And Meredith runs low and fast, with the singular determination that only she can bring.

Pack.

Pack fight.

A fist punches up in the darkness of the inside of the armoured van, with a surge of energy pulsing through Reginald who drives his hand through the wall of mud and stones to feel the void of an empty space.

And in that same second, with the bandage around his head now ripped off, Cookey lies on his back with that feeling of falling slowing and stopping, until it reverses and feels like he's surging up faster and faster. His heart going like the clappers. His whole body thrumming with energy, and those startling, twinkling, magical blue eyes snap open.

The same eyes as the five-year-old boy that was frozen in fear.

But Cookey isn't five anymore.

He's the scariest motherfucker in this place, and the violence explodes as *The Ketchup Song* drifts across the town, and he sinks his teeth into the clown's neck. Tearing the artery open, with hot blood spurting into his face.

'FUCK YOU!' he roars out and angles the clown for the blood to spray into the eyes of another one lunging in, making it blink and flinch as that low streak of angry, wet fur and focussed determination runs like the wind between Danny and Mo while exerting her will to them all.

Pack.

Pack fight.

A pulse inside. Cookey surges up, his eyes wide with

pure violent fury as Meredith flies inside the tent to take the heavy female clown down, and like the grenade that Paula used, Cookey detonates right there inside that tent.

His pistol dropped, but he draws his knife and slams it into the stomach of a clown trying to get up, and he saws hard, tearing the flesh open. Then he pulls the knife out and stabs behind into another one, and stamps down on a knee joint. Snapping the leg. He turns and headbutts another one down, then drops it to stab it in the neck. One slams into his side, but Cookey cries out in pure frenzied pleasure and bites an ear off with his teeth then a nose, and a cheek while stabbing and killing. Roaring with violence as the clowns attack only to die, and in the van, buried under the cliff, Reginald's hand finds something hard to grip and use to pull himself up. Rising inch by inch. Kicking and thrashing his legs. His lungs desperate to suck air in. The mud trying to pull him back down, but he fights and kicks as the tugboat nears the shore, and those inside start throwing tools and chains onto the beach.

Danny, Mo, Charlie, and Jess laying waste to their horde. Charlie using the mallet. Danny and Mo using knives to stab and cut throats. Danny with brutal power and strength, and Mo dancing and weaving like Dave. Fluid like water. Flowing without effort.

Cookey inside. Ripping the entrails out from a stomach to wrap around a neck and rip a fat clown off his feet before standing back, and swinging the intestines over his head like a cowboy at a rodeo.

'COME ON!' he roars out and kicks the one-armed clown with dwarfism into several more, before he whips at them using the innards, but it's not enough. It's not close enough. Cookey needs more. He needs to feel their bones in his hands after nearly two decades of pure terror from what they did to him, and he dives in with his knife. Stabbing and cutting, and crawling on his hands and knees over their bodies. Hacking them apart.

While in the suffocating confines of the van Reginald's lungs near burst with the desire to draw air as he pulls himself up. But it's not enough. He can't do it. He starts sinking but feels the steering wheel beneath his feet. He kicks down. Hitting the horn that still works.

'He's alive!' Carmen shouts in the tug. Hearing the noise muffled under tonnes of mud, and she leaps over the bow to land in the water and half swim, and half wade to the shore and crawls, then runs out while shouting his name. 'HOLD ON, REGINALD! WE'RE COMING!'

But Reginald can't hear them. He's too busy not dying today. No, thank you. No, sir. Not today, if you please, and he pulls and kicks, and rams his already sore head into that wall again and again until it eventually breaks apart, and he surges up into the void to draw glorious air into his lungs.

Which is at the exact same second that Cookey hacks into the rib cage of a clown with enough force to get a hand in to clamp onto the lungs as they fill with blood. 'Breathe in my face now, motherfucker,' he snarls into the twisted, dying, painted face then hacks down into the neck and through the flesh and bone, and stands up to prise the head free of the body to hold aloft. Shouting out in victory. Blood pouring down every inch of his face as the clowns rally and come at him, and he yells in delight and clubs one down using the decapitated head and launches into full on Clarence berserker mode. Kicking and stamping with intestines and innards wrapped around his arm.

Two hit into him. Taking him off his feet. Cookey twists and laughs, and bites into a neck while pushing his thumbs into the other one's eyes before sliding over one body to bite into that one. Then he's up and throwing another one over his hip and breaking its arms and legs with the skills learned over a month of solid fighting, because he's not that little boy anymore.

And on the beach, Carmen grabs one of the thrown pickaxes and climbs the mud towards the sound of the horn to start hacking into it, but that rain still falls. Making it hard and wet, and dangerous.

While inside, Reginald feels above to another hard thing and uses it to grip and pull. Another above it. Like the rungs of ladder. But Reginald is smart, and he knows they're not rungs, but he still uses them as such and gasps, and drags his body free as the world around him starts to tremble and shake with more of the cliff starting to come down.

'CARMEN!' Henry shouts. 'GET DOWN!'

Carmen pauses to look back and dives down the mound as more of the cliff starts to collapse. Sending tonnes more mud and collapsing down with an awful roaring noise, and burying the horse trailer completely.

Carmen heaves for air at the base. They all do. Staring on in horror as the landslide comes to a stop. 'Go!' Carmen shouts, grabbing her pickaxe to start climbing back up.

'Not up!' Nick shouts as they all look at him. 'Don't dig down. Dig through. Right there,' he adds and points to the wall of mud in front, and starts attacking it with a pickaxe. A fraction of a second for the others to pause before running to join him. Clarence with one hand still hitting the mound harder than anyone else using two.

Reginald gasps inside, climbing higher to the top of his void and using the rungs to brace his feet while reaching out to feel the hard protrusion above jutting out, and the cliff collapses again. Roaring past him as he grits his teeth and clings on within the space he's found.

Howie, Paula, Marcy, and Dave cut them down, with Tappy using the Saxon to kill swathes at a time, and the surface waters run red with blood while the feeble, old man in Rye holds his manhood cheap. Sobbing in fear while listening to people fight so that survivors like he might live.

Cookey in the tent. Slaughtering many with his bare hands.

Charlie, Danny, and Mo outside, doing the same.

Nick on the beach, digging into the landslide. All of them digging and clawing the mud away to tunnel inwards, ignoring the cliff still coming down around them. They heave for air and dig because Nick told them to.

Reginald inside. Gripping on for dear life as the mud pours down around him. He slips and drops from his fingerless left hand not being able to grip, but he cries out and gets his foot onto a rung, and rises again, because that's what they do. They rise and rise and, never back down.

'Why are we going in and not down?' Carmen asks.

Nick saves his breath for digging. Heaving the mud away after his own brain, unique in its own powers, calculated the trajectory of the drop the van would have taken having seen the position of the horse trailer.

Which is why he aims this way and keeps the others going to make a tunnel while Reginald feels the mud rising around his feet again, and Cookey tears the still beating heart from a clown's chest and shoves it down the clown's throat.

'Nick!' Carmen yells. 'We have to go down...'

But she cuts off when Nick's pickaxe strikes metal. 'Here!' Nick grunts, and they all work on the spot. Tearing the mud away.

'We've got something,' Maddox shouts to Henry in the tug, holding the boat off from being beached.

'It's the van!' Carmen says, seeing the upper corner of the back doors.

'Dig down. Hurry,' Nick orders as they keep going. Digging down to get beneath the back doors and deeper still. 'That's it! Chains. We need the chains!'

Clarence runs back to wade through the deep water and heave himself over into the boat, with Henry pulling him in, and the two of them handling the impossibly heavy chain to get them over Clarence's shoulder. He drops back over the side into the sea with the weight of the chains taking Clarence beneath the surface. The others cry out and rush in to help him, but he surges up and powers out. Dragging the chain over to Nick flying flat and motioning to pass the end, so he can hook it to the van's tow bar.

A moment of fumbling and cursing. A moment in which the cliff collapses again, with more than before slamming down. Making them all run backwards. Clarence grabbing at Nick's foot to pull him away.

'NO! Wait,' Nick yells and fumbles to get the hook latched on, then shouts he's done it, and feels himself being bodily lifted and thrown clear as the cliff comes down and buries the van and chain again. Reginald inside. Feeling it happen. Clinging on for dear life.

'NOW!' Nick shouts, on his feet and waving his arms at Henry who pushes the lever forward for the propellers of the powerful engines to bite into the water and drive the strong tug out into the sea. The chain pings straight, and the engines whine louder as Henry applies more power.

For a second, nothing seems to happen, but the will exerted wins through, and the mound of mud shifts as the van is slowly pulled out. The angle righting her onto her broken wheels, with the front coming down hard.

'MORE! KEEP GOING!' Nick yells, waving at Henry to go further. 'STOP, STOP, STOP!'

Henry kills the power, and they swarm to wrench the doors open. Using tools to lever them as Clarence heaves the broken sliding door open, only for that fear to come back at the wet mud inside pouring out.

'Dig into it!' Carmen shouts, grabbing a spade to start heaving it out, but the others know there is no way Reginald could have survived in that.

It's just not physically possible.

'Come on, dig!' she yells at the others not doing anything.

'Carmen,' Nick calls.

'Just fucking dig!' she yells.

'Carmen!' Frank snaps. His voice driving into her head and making her look back with a snarl before she spots them all staring past her. She whips her head around then staggers back at the sight.

'Holy fucking fuck,' she mouths, not believing the sight. Not believing it for one second, and if anyone ever said such a thing could happen, she would say no and refuse to believe it.

But there it is.

There *he* is.

Reginald.

Inside the rib cage of a giant dinosaur, with his spine pressing to the creature's once long and wide, powerful back bone. His feet wedged into the ribs like rungs. His hands stretched up to clutch the lower jawbone, with the blood coming out of his severed fingers to drip down the dinosaur's chin like it's still alive and feasting.

'I would suggest this is a new species as otherwise yet unknown,' Reginald says from inside the creature that kept him alive. 'Judging by the size and structure, that is, and one would also suggest this is perhaps the most intact remains found ever in this region, most likely the whole country.'

They don't speak.

They can't.

The sight of it.

The sight of Reginald still in his shirt and tie, covered in mud and dripping blood from his hand and head, who then promptly faints as they cry out and rush in as Charlie slams the mallet down and winces at the spray of blood splatting her face as the head explodes.

Danny and Mo heaving for air nearby. The fight is over, but the rain still pours, soaking them all, and they still don't know where Cookey is.

But Jess turns.

Sensing sound and motion and moving forward through the rain with Charlie on her back. Seeing the big tent loom into view. Charlie gasps at being so close, and she slides off the saddle to rush inside but freezes at the sight of Cookey inside, laying waste to the clowns around him.

Destroying them one at a time with vicious, brutal ease.

Tearing a man's leg off and using it to kill others.

Blood spraying in the air.

Cookey snapping necks and limbs, with blood pouring down his jaw that suggests he's bitten throats out.

He takes the last one down and drops to grab a fallen knife, then hacks away until he stands back, holding the decapitated head by the dyed orange hair.

Something about him.

Something so very different.

An intensity she's seen before.

An aura pouring off him.

He looks older. Harder. Not a lad, but a man.

And when he turns, she notices the injured eye is still swollen, and the other looks red.

She blinks at the blood on him. On his jaw and neck, and down his front. Coated on his arms, and she blinks again at the decapitated head of a clown held in one hand, with entrails wrapped around his wrist.

A glance past him to the sea of corpses inside the tent. Broken bodies, shredded and torn apart.

All of them killed by Cookey walking towards her. Not speaking. Not saying anything. A look about him that sends a thrill inside of her from the savage intensity coming from him. The way his chest heaves. The way he moves. Like an apex predator.

Like Blowers after he died saving Maddox and the baby.

Like Howie after he had the heart pushing into his mouth in the car park.

Like Nick when he fought alone to save the children and Lilly's brother.

The sight of him holds Charlie still. Her face covered in blood. Her body too. Her clothes soaked and clinging to her frame. Showing her shape, and the outline of her breasts clear in the wet top. She breathes harder. Her eyes fixed on his as he throws the head to one side and flings the entrails away before rushing into her. His bloodied hand taking the back of her bloodied neck as they press their bloodied lips together, and the thunder booms overhead, making the ground tremble and shake as they kiss.

Their bodies touching.

Their mouths locked.

And that kiss becomes passionate and the most charged, erotic, sensual moment of Charlie's life.

A moment seared between them.

A moment only for them, and every doubt and seed of confusion in Charlie vanishes as she feels the energy and love pouring into her, and that energy becomes stronger and charged, and his hands touch her body. Her hips. Her back. Her neck.

It should last forever, and if heaven exists, then this would be it, but slowly.

Ever so slowly.

He pulls back, and the contact drifts apart, with an immediate sense of loss felt in both, but all things *must* end.

Nothing can last forever, and she opens her eyes to look into his as he whispers. 'Michael Bublé.'

She bursts out laughing with a sound that does not belong in that place of death and ruin, but the prize goes to the victors, and in this brave, new world, they are the winners.

11

THEY MEET WHERE THEY SPLIT UP.

Inside The Ship Inn, the survivors stare down at the bodies floating in the shallows or lying mangled and broken everywhere else.

'Look,' someone whispers, pointing to a vessel coming into view out of the rain.

'And there,' someone else says as the people angle to see down to the squat military vehicle rumbling to a stop below them.

Five people get out.

Four of them wearing hats taken from the hat shop.

The same style and colour as the one Marcy grabbed to keep her hair out of her eyes.

Military style pink berets tugged stylishly down at one side.

The tug berths clumsily as the figures inside clamber over the side to grapple with ropes to secure her to the mooring posts.

'Jesus, look,' another survivor whispers from a side window as they all rush over to see a horse coming slowly into view through the rain. Two people on the horse. A man and woman. Two young men either side. One small and Arabic. One tall and black.

All four of them wearing Stetson hats, taken from the hat shop they found while searching for the others.

All four of them puffing on big, fat Cuban cigars, taken from another shop nearby.

But that's not the thing that makes the survivors mutter and gasp. It's the sight of the huge dog walking next to them, with a clown leg in its mouth, with the oversized boot still on the foot.

The horse comes to a stop. The four people stay put. The dog too.

The people from the military vehicle stand still too.

Four of them wearing pink berets.

One of them not wearing a pink beret.

The people from the boat splash over and come to a stop, clustered protectively around a small man covered in mud, with his left hand wrapped in gaffer tape. A black woman close at his side.

A second of silence as the three groups stare at each other before the first voice floats up.

'Try getting out the van *before* it falls of a cliff next time, Reggie,' a beautiful woman in a pink beret says.

'Yes, Marcy.'

'What happened to your hand?' she asks.

'A dinosaur bit his fingers off,' a tall, young man says.

'Nick, stop being a twat,' the beautiful woman says.

'My fingers were shorn off by the van door closing. It just *appeared* the dinosaur did it.'

Silence for a second as the rain lashes down.

'Did you just say shorn?' Marcy asks. 'Were they *shorn* off, were they?'

'Oh, bugger off, Marcy,' Reginald huffs.

'Hang on. A dinosaur?' Howie asks.

'Reggie was inside the dinosaur that was inside the cliff,' Nick says as everyone shrugs and figures that sounds perfectly normal. 'But whoa. More importantly. Why haven't we got hats?'

'Or cigars,' Blower says.

'We got you hats,' Tappy says, holding a big box full of more berets.

'And we got you cigars,' Cookey says as Danny inhales his and bends over in a coughing fit. 'Danny, seriously, don't inhale.'

'I forgot!' Danny gasps as the three groups merge and melt into one, with pink berets and cigars being passed around while everyone makes a fuss of the small, muddy man and his gaffer-taped hand. Hugging and kissing him. Patting his back and shoulders. Shaking his right hand and lighting a cigar for him.

'Don't inhale it,' Cookey says as Danny starts coughing again.

'I forgot again,' he wheezes as Paula rubs his back, and Marcy removes his Stetson to pull a pink beret onto his head.

'Why pink?' Nick asks.

'No idea,' Tappy says. 'They must have had a job lot for a fancy dress party or something. Ha! You look awesome.'

'Yeah?' Nick asks, tugging his over, with a cigar between his teeth. 'And what happened to you two?' he asks as they all turn to Cookey and Charlie.

'We found 'em snogging by the tent,' Mo says.

'You did not find us snogging by the tent,' Charlie tries to say, but it's too late as the jeers go up.

'You were snogging while we were working our arses off?' Nick asks.

'We were not snogging! We had one kiss,' Charlie says, which really doesn't help matters. 'But what was that music playing?'

'The Ketchup Song!' Tappy says with a laugh.

'I heard that!' Paula says. 'I was like... *what the actual?*'

'The music player thing got knocked,' Tappy says.

'The what song?' Nick asks.

'The Ketchup Song,' Tappy says as he looks blank. 'Nick! Seriously.'

'There's a song about ketchup? What like from an advert?' Nick asks.

'Even I know what that song is,' Henry says.

'Jesus, Nick,' Cookey says. '*I say a-hee haa a-hedity haa.*' he sings to the tune, doing the dance by waving one open hand over the other in turn.

'Fuck off, really?' Blowers asks, seeing Nick still looking confused.

'Play it again,' Cookey says, with Tappy rolling her eyes in mock awe that someone could possibly not know the song.

'The dance?' Cookey says, doing it again as Tappy hits repeat, and the jaunty tune once again blasts from the loudspeakers, with nearly all of them humming along and doing the hand over hand dance.

'Oh! I know this!' Nick says with delight, bobbing his head and bringing his hands up to swing one over the other.

'They're fucking nuts,' one of the survivors looking down from the building whispers as they all look to the dozen or so people in pink berets smoke cigars while doing the hand dance to *The Ketchup Song* while the giant dog jumps into the back of the military vehicle with a severed leg.

'I feel sick. Can I put it out please?' Danny asks when the music stops as he holds the cigar away.

'Yeah, bro. They're gross,' Mo says, pulling a face.

'Yes, they're really not pleasant, are they,' Charlie says as they all ditch them into the deep puddles around their feet, with Dave, looking pointedly from them to the bin a few feet away.

'Sorry, Dave,' Howie says, grabbing his soggy cigar from the puddle to throw in the bin.

'Sorry, Dave,' the others say, doing the same after getting *the look*.

'Keep Britain tidy,' Dave tells them.

'Why aren't you wearing a hat, Dave?' Mo asks.

'He wouldn't wear one,' Marcy says.

'A beret is a thing of significance to a military man,' Henry says. 'It determines loyalty to regiment.'

'You mean military *person*,' Paula corrects.

'Of course. A military person' Henry says with his charming smile as he and Frank pull their sand-coloured SAS berets from pockets to tug on, and Carmen finds her dark green SBS beret, but she pauses, looking at it and frowning for a second.

'I like the pink better,' she says, putting hers away and smiling at Reginald in his pink hat.

Henry notices the metaphorical steps Carmen takes as she seeks independence from his team. But he shows no reaction.

'Well. We are now the Mr Howie Pink Tesco Regiment,' Marcy says.

'Indeed, but I think you mean the Mr Howie *and* Paula regiment,' Henry says.

'You are so smooth, Henry!' Paula says with a laugh, kissing his cheek with a quick hug, which again makes Henry pause because Major Henry Dillington-Campbell doesn't *do* hugs. He's not the hugging type at all. What a strange, new world this is.

'Yeah, on the subject of military and all that stuff,' Howie says. They all fall silent at his serious tone as a voice calls out behind them from one of the upper windows.

'Er, hello? Sorry, but are you the army?'

'Hold that sentence,' Paula says to Howie as she turns and starts towards the building.

'I've got it,' Cookey says, waving her back with a gentle smile, and he turns to stride through the rain. 'Hi! Are you all okay? Anybody hurt in there?'

Paula frowns. Sensing the thing that Charlie saw. That different energy coming from Cookey who suddenly seems less lad and more man.

'Did you two really kiss?' Tappy asks her quietly.

Charlie nods, staring after Cookey. 'He got trapped in a tent with some clowns.'

'Fuck,' Blowers says as the others frown, knowing how terrified Cookey is.

'Did you get him out?' Nick asks.

'No. I did not,' Charlie says quietly. 'He *John Wick'd* them. Meredith didn't pull that leg off. Cookey did, and he came out holding a decapitated clown head.'

'We have a medic if you do need help, but er, otherwise you need to get your supplies together and head to the fort. It's only a few miles down the coast,' Cookey calls up as they all stare after him. All of them standing in the hard rain, wearing berets.

All apart from one.

'What were you going to say?' Paula asks Howie.

'I was about to say Henry needs to take command. Marcy just said it. I worked at Tesco. I would have jumped down that cliff after Reggie and gotten us all killed.'

'Just hang on a second,' Paula says.

'I'm being serious. And it's not a sulky thing either. We're over that. I mean, Henry and I are over that. He takes command. He's trained for this.'

'Nobody is *trained* for this, Howie,' Paula says.

'But Henry's skills are the closest we need. What was that thing he said? What was that thing you said?'

'What thing?' Henry asks.

'We plan and think and…'

'We plan. We think. We succeed,' Henry says.

'That,' Howie says, motioning to Henry while looking to Paula then to Clarence. 'I don't do that. I just charge in. That's my only skill.'

'It's got you this far,' Paula says.

'Yeah, and now it's time for the professional to lead,' Howie says, holding his hands up to show his sincerity. But like Carmen always said, that's the endearing thing about Howie – he wears his heart on his sleeve, and they can all see he genuinely means what he says without any hint of malice or spite, and to a degree, it does make sense.

But only to a degree, which is something Henry does see, with his greater years of experience.

'I accept,' Henry says as Howie nods, and Paula frowns. 'Partially,' Henry adds as even Cookey turns to listen. 'Granted. I can plan and strategize, but I would have retreated when your instinct was to attack and go forward which, in turn, would have delayed us too long to reach Reginald. And I would have retreated at Gatwick and Crawley, and the many other places. I agree that you cannot do what I can do, Howie. But that works both ways. Your instincts *in* battle are far greater than mine. So I propose, going forward, that we work on a *three-tier* system. Reginald will guide us with consultation to where we need to be. I will then ensure we get to that place and plan accordingly, and once there, Howie will assume command... And no doubt, kick the shit out of everyone in his path to make sure we all survive.'

Snorts of laughter. The energy spiking and flowing between them. Howie's dark eyes showing the humour as Henry holds a hand out. 'Agreed?' Henry asks.

'Agreed,' Howie says as they both turn to hold hands out to Reginald.

'Sorry chaps, but my fingers have been shorn off,' Reginald says, shaking one at a time as the silence extends for a second.

'Really had to use shorn again there, didn't you,' Marcy says.

'Shorn is a perfectly good verb, Marcy!'

'Er, sorry!' the survivor who called out shouts from the window, making them all turn to look up. 'But there's one of the things over there.'

He points towards the river to an infected in a yellow sailing bib, falling over the side of a yacht beached on the shore and splashing up to his feet.

A flurry of pistols drawn, with dull clicks sounding out one after the other.

'Bollocks, I'm out,' Nick says,

'I'm out,' Booker says, lowering his empty pistol as the rest all do the same.

'Dave?' Howie asks.

'Yes, Mr Howie.'

'Jesus, Dave. You know what I'm going to ask.'

'What, Mr Howie?'

'He does it on purpose! You do it on purpose.'

'Dave, do you have any bullets left?' Marcy asks.

'No, Marcy.'

'Thank you, Dave,' she says while giving Howie a look.

'None of us have any rounds left in our pistols,' Dave says. 'Mr Howie fired his last one outside the hat shop, and Paula fired her last one before she used my second to last grenade.'

'I knew you'd have another one,' Paula says.

'The only person that has a bullet left is Marcy. She fired sixteen rounds. Her sidearm has a capacity for seventeen rounds.'

'Really?' Marcy asks, drawing her pistol to slide the magazine out. 'Oh, he's right. I've got one left.'

'Give it to Dave,' Howie says.

'Why?'

'So he can shoot the zombie!'

'Not zombies,' Reginald says as Marcy slots the magazine in and slides the top back to chamber the round before holding it out to Dave, but she frowns and pulls it back with a wry smile, and steps out to lift her arm and aim at the infected, still a good eighty metres away.

'No way,' Paula says, shaking her head.

'She might get it,' Carmen says. 'Marcy's got a steady arm.'

'Thank you, Carmen,' Marcy says.

'Get off,' Frank says.

'Not a chance,' Blowers says.

'I'm backing you, Marcy,' Carmen says.

'I'm bloody not,' Paula says with a laugh.

'Dave?' Marcy asks. 'Do you think I can shoot that infected from here?'

'No, Marcy.'

'So, if I do, then it will be a good shot, right?'

'Yes, Marcy.'

'Would it be worthy of a prize?'

'What prize?' Dave asks.

'Hmmm. Tell you what. If I shoot that infected from here, then we all have to agree to wear our pink berets for a week.'

'Is that it?' Paula asks.

'Henry and Frank too,' Marcy says to smiles and looks to Henry and Frank rolling their eyes.

'She'll never hit him from here,' Frank says.

'Henry?' Marcy asks.

'I'll take those odds, Marcy.'

'Go on, Marcy,' Carmen says. 'Steady arm. Breathe slowly. Relax and squeeze the trigger. And aim just over his head because of the rain.'

Marcy steadies herself and whispers one last question. 'And you, Dave? If I hit that infected, you have to wear a pink beret for a week.'

All eyes on Dave.

The small, quiet man that rarely shows reaction or emotion, but there, in the rain, they all swear there's a very gentle tug of his lips.

'Yes, Marcy.'

She fires, and the last bullet of the Battle for Rye flies through the air.

12

A single shot rings out. The sharp crack somewhat muted in the heavy rain, and less than a third of a second later, the last infected still standing after the battle for Rye falls backwards into the river.

'Shot,' Carmen says with a nod of appreciation.

'What happened? Did he fall over?' Marcy asks.

'No! You shot him.'

'I shot him?'

'Yes.'

'With this gun?' Marcy asks with a quick look to Dave to make sure he hadn't fired a shot without her seeing. 'Oh. My. God.'

'Told you Marcy's got a good eye,' Carmen says as the rest of them mentally catch up to what just happened.

'No fucking way,' Blowers says.

'Shot,' Nick says in awe.

'Jesus, Marcy. Well done,' Tappy says.

'I got him. I actually got him,' Marcy says as Dave starts walking off. 'Er. Where are you going?'

'To check.'

'To check what?' Marcy asks, rushing after him as they all do the same and start splashing through the ankle-deep waters.

'Do not tell me you're checking my kill,' Marcy says as Dave peers down at the now dead undead and looks at the neat little scorched entry wound in the centre of the forehead, and notes the back of the skull and bits of brains spattered in the waters behind the body. 'Did I get him then?' Marcy says, pushing into Dave's side.

'Yes,' Dave says.

'Ha! Yes!' Marcy says, wrapping an arm round Dave's shoulders and planting a kiss on his cheek. 'Winner, winner, turkey something meat dinner,' she sing-songs.

'Chicken dinner,' Mo tells her.

'Chicken dinner,' she sings.

'I wish we had a chicken dinner,' Nick says wistfully as the others gather around to check the kill they didn't quite believe either while Marcy tugs a pink beret from her pocket and shows it to Dave with a smile. But it's her genuine smile and not the big movie star smile this time. The one that's almost a bit lopsided.

'We made a deal,' she tells Dave.

'What deal?'

'Don't you even. That might work with Howie, but don't even try it with me. And I know you hate being touched, but I'm going to put it on you. Okay?'

'Okay,' Dave says. His voice as flat as ever. Devoid of emotion while somehow conveying tolerance. And Howie notices that Dave doesn't flinch when Marcy comes in close and tugs it on his head, then stands back with a smile.

'Now we're all the same,' she tells him. 'One of Mr Howie's Tesco Regiment.'

'Ahem,' Paula says.

'One of Mr Howie's *and Paula's* Tesco Regiment,' Marcy says without breaking her smile. 'I would say Henry too, but he's not wearing the proud pink,' she adds with a glance at Henry and Frank in their sand-coloured SAS berets. 'Even though we did all make a deal,' she says pointedly as they roll their eyes before swiping their SAS berets off to replace them with the pink ones Marcy handed out.

'They're very good quality, actually,' Paula says, fingering hers. 'And they feel waterproof.'

'Quality berets are waterproof,' Henry says as Dave reaches up to tug his over and shape it with his hands until it starts resembling the style of Henry and Frank's, and not the puffed-up mini chef hats everyone else has.

'Ooh, do mine,' Marcy says, ducking her head for Dave to reach up and tug, and shape hers, and again, Howie watches on. Seeing the familiarity between them, and how Dave is allowing social touch, but then, Marcy has developed a way with Dave. Howie doesn't know how Marcy can do that. He keeps thinking to ask, but there never seems to be enough time.

The others quickly join in copying them while Howie stands to the side. Taking it all in and sweeping his eyes over the quaint, old town of Rye. Not that it's very quaint after they've finished with it. Especially not the village green place where the visiting circus had been camped with their big, striped tent that Cookey got trapped in with a bunch of clowns, of which he is terrified.

But then, these days are not the old days, and as it turns out, the clowns should have feared *him* far more than Cookey feared them.

Charlie saw the last few minutes of it.

She said he tore them apart with his bare hands.

She said she saw him rip a fully grown man's leg from a body and use it to beat more to death.

She said when he walked out, his eyes were red, and he was holding a decapitated head.

She said he was like a demon.

She said he had this dark powerful energy pouring off him.

She said, '*He was like you, Mr Howie.*'

Howie didn't quite know what that meant. The others knew exactly what that meant, and they all looked over to Cookey a few metres away, calling up to the survivors barricaded in the building alongside the river. He seemed different. Harder. Tougher. Less cheeky lad, and more charming man instead.

'Told you she was a good shot,' Carmen says.

Howie smiles at the gentle play and the energy flowing between them. All of them exhausted to the bone and covered in so much gaffer tape it looks like they were inside an exploding tape factory. But it's been relentless since they set out yesterday morning.

Was it yesterday? Howie thinks. He doesn't know when it was. Or when they last slept properly or ate properly, or even had a coffee. He couldn't even say what day it is, or how many days it has been since the outbreak started. It's all a blur. All of it. The whole thing.

'We should move out,' Howie starts to say as someone calls out, and they turn to see the survivors edging out into the rain.

'Er. I said hello?' a podgy woman at the front snaps in a demanding tone.

'Sorry, what?' Howie asks.

'I've been stood here shouting for you!'

'It's raining. I couldn't hear you,' Howie says.

'Where's our transport,' the woman shouts over him.

'Eh?'

'Transport! That soldier promised there would be transport for this fort place.'

'I didn't,' Cookey says. 'I said *you* need to find transport.'

'Er. Excuse me!' she says in a triggered voice. 'We are civilians.'

'You're the bloody army!' a man at her side snaps. 'You're meant to do this.'

'Do what?' Howie asks.

'It's your job to get us out of here!' the woman yells. 'And where the hell have you been? We've been trapped in there for a month! We've had to ration our food!'

'Not that much by the looks of it,' Howie says before he can stop himself.

'I BEG YOUR PARDON!' the woman shouts.

'I want your name!' the guy next to her shouts. 'And your commanding officer.'

'How dare you!' the woman yells.

'We've just killed them all for you!' Howie shouts, taking a step as Clarence grabs his arm to pull him back.

'Howie, don't,' Paula says. 'We're armed. They aren't.'

'I wasn't bloody armed when this happened,' Howie says. 'I had a hammer that got stuck in someone's head. Seriously. I'm fed up with these entitled pricks.'

'Howie, just stop it,' Paula says.

'I won't bloody stop it.'

'Five people died waiting for you!' the angry woman shouts, which only ignites the already short fuse as Howie detonates.

'You didn't lose five waiting for us, you fucking fucker! You lost five while you justified your cowardice and kept stuffing your faces! How did they even die? You were locked inside?'

'They were elderly! They didn't have their medication.'

'There's a fucking chemist in the town!' Howie yells back at her.

'Fuck's sake, Donna. Just shut up!' another woman yells at the large, angry woman. 'Sorry, how do we get out of here?' she asks with a desperate look to Howie and the others.

'Do not tell me to shut up, Linda!' Donna shouts, incensed at losing her control and the lack of respect being shown to her obvious leadership. 'I've kept us all alive!'

'You didn't keep us alive!' Linda yells back at her. 'You kept us too scared to speak out by hiding the food while Jim threatened us with that fucking shotgun. You fucking bitch! YOU FUCKING BITCH!' she yells out, now free to vent the fear and panic, and rage suppressed inside at Donna and Jim forcing everyone else to do what they said, and she lunges at Donna. Punching her full in the face and grabbing a fistful of hair as Donna slaps out, and they tussle and scream at the same time as an older guy throws a weak punch at Jim who pushes him over, with all hell breaking loose. Children crying, and more men going for Jim, and more women kicking and grabbing at Donna.

'That's enough!' Paula says, trying to get Linda off Donna and getting slapped by a stray hand as the others wade in. Pulling them apart amidst the shouts and screams.

'String the bitch up!' another angry woman shouts, spitting at Donna as Maddox lifts her away with an arm around her waist, and Booker does the same to another one with his arm wrapped around her chest.

'Do you want your shotgun back, Jim?' the old man Jim pushed over yells as he lurches out of the building aiming a double-barrelled shotgun, and the shouts go up as Dave draws a knife, knowing he has no rounds left in his pistol.

'Put it down now!' Frank shouts, aiming his empty assault rifle at the elderly fellow who yells out and pulls the trigger with a deafening boom, and Jim flies off his feet in a shower of blood as Dave throws the knife, skewering the man through the neck as Carmen darts in from the side and punches him down while wrenching the shotgun out of his hands.

And the screams and dying, and murder, and outrage from the old times carry on once more in this brave, new world while Reginald watches on. Seeing it all, and more besides.

13

Roy says he knows a place.

The Fat Bee Garden Centre on the A22. Remote and isolated, and with high fencing to deter rural burglaries. He said it's also got a decent sized café and an outdoor equipment store inside.

It takes time to organise the survivors, but strangely, after the old fellow shot Jim and Donna ran off screaming into the town, fearing she'd be lynched, the remaining people seemed more motivated to get going.

I stayed away from them and helped wash the mud off the crates off ammunition they'd dragged from the armoured van, so we could reload our rifles and pistols, enough to get us out the shit in case of another contact. Henry and Paula dealt with the survivors and found them minibuses and vans to load into with instructions on the best route while the people faffed around and moaned about everything.

'Why aren't you escorting us?' someone asked.

We didn't bother trying to explain that we're not actually allowed inside our own fucking fort due to Lilly and the travellers pointing guns at us to make Henry tell them where the Panacea was. Which, in turn, prompted Henry to swiftly execute their leaders and then install George as the fort's new Fuhrer or puppet master, or whatever the shit he's called. I don't care. I don't care about the fort, and I don't care about the whining survivors either.

What I care about is my team, and that's the other reason for not escorting them. We've been on our feet and fighting solidly for over thirty-six hours without decent refs.

We need sleep.

We set off slowly, so Jess can keep up without pushing her too hard. The Saxon and the Royal Mail van trundling along until we reach the A22 and make the first stop at the Golden Cross Equestrian Centre to find a new horsebox.

We pull up and drop out to see Jess fidgeting and rearing her head back in way we all know means something is wrong.

'Infected?' I ask, thinking the last thing we need right now is another fight, but Charlie shakes her head.

'I don't think so. Meredith isn't growling. She can probably smell dead horses,' she says and nods to the big building housing the stores and offices, a sand-school, and internal stables.

I exhale slowly at the grim realisation and the prospect of seeing dead creatures, left locked in to suffer and die in the heat without water.

But we need a horsebox, and there are plenty of them here. Only problem, of course, is that the keys are all inside that big building.

'You stay outside,' I tell Charlie and start forward.

Clarence and Dave go with me. Henry follows us. The others ranging out to watch the sides.

We head inside through the foyer and the looted bar. The stench already ripe. Coming from the back. We know what we'll find, but we check it anyway. The *what if* is too strong and hangs in the air.

What if an animal is still alive?

What if someone needs help.

They're not, and there isn't.

We find them in the stalls. Foals and ponies. A few miniature horses. All of them dead and reduced to carcasses, already eaten down to the bones. Millions of flies in the air, and rats scurrying and squeaking in alarm at being disturbed.

That darkness seeps into my mind again. That someone took the time to steal money and booze from the looted bar but not open stalls to let the horses out.

They would have died slowly too. From thirst. From hunger. From the heat.

'Don't dwell on it,' Henry says, reading my expression, but I clock he looks as grim as me and Clarence. 'We need to focus on those we *can* save.'

We head back out to see Nick and Roy already attaching a robust looking horse box trailer thing to the back of the Royal Mail van, and Tappy looting the tack shop. Taking straps and buckles, and even saddles.

'What do you need saddles for?' I ask.

'Thick leather,' she says with an awkward glance to Clarence. 'I, er, I was thinking about your hand or the stump, and like, covering it or making a thing to put on the end?'

'Prosthetic?' Charlie calls while helping to attach the horsebox.

'Yeah. One of those,' Tappy says, blinking up at Clarence. 'I mean. If that's okay. I didn't want to just assume or...'

'It's fine,' Clarence says in his deep, rumbling voice ,and even through the exhaustion, I can see he feels touched at the gesture. 'Thank you, Natasha.'

She beams a quick, tired smile and shoves it into the side of the van while Jess gets coaxed inside the new horsebox.

Then we're off again. Just a short hop down the road to the A22 Animal Feed Store in Lower Dicker. A name that would normally prompt a whole day's worth of jokes and banter, but Cookey doesn't even mention it. Nobody does.

The feed store is an old building at the entrance to a trading estate filled with engineering workshops and prefabricated units used for vehicle repairs and MOT testing.

We drop out into the rain once again, feeling more exhausted by the minute. Our mood and energy low.

I get a smoke from Nick, but the cigarette becomes soggy within seconds from the rain pouring down my face. I ditch it in the gutter and watch it floating off towards the drain. The lads do the same. Then we all turn to see Dave staring from us to a litter bin no more than six feet away.

'Didn't see it,' I tell him.

I don't know if he buys my fib. It's impossible to tell with Dave, and he's still the only one of us without a mark on him.

No. That's not true. His clothes are dirty and spattered with blood and gore, but it's not *his* blood or gore. He doesn't have a scratch on him. Not a single wound.

It's insane how he can go through something like that and not let a single infected get close enough to mark him, and yet that same man still thinks it's important to put rubbish in bins that will never get emptied.

I hear a tut and look over to Clarence standing behind Carmen trying to break the lock on the pet food place. She steps aside when he waves his stump at her before using one of his massive feet to remove the whole door from the frame.

We grab bags of oats and new feeding buckets, seeing that Jess has a habit of smashing them to bits straight after eating. Then Carmen uses her knife to start splitting open the big bags of animal food to spill seeds and mealworms, and oats all over the floor.

'For the local wildlife,' she says when we look over at her.

'Shouldn't we put it outside?' Danny asks.

'Leave it in the dry,' she tells him.

'How will they find it?'

'They'll find it,' Carmen replies. She normally explains things when Danny and Mo ask. It's obvious she *likes* teaching them about birds and wildlife, but there just isn't anything left in us.

'We done?' Paula asks, clearly impatient to reach this garden centre, and no doubt, knowing we've got a whole lot of work left to do before we can even think about sleeping.

'I need to feed Jess,' Charlie says.

'Do at the garden centre,' Paula says. 'Roy said it's just up the road.'

'What if we get another contact? Jess hasn't eaten for a day.'

'None of us have.'

'She's a horse, Paula! She's five times bigger than Clarence. She needs to eat!' Charlie says in a voice edging quickly towards anger.

'Okay! Fine,' Paula says, flapping a hand to show she's backing down. 'Just get it done.'

I watch Charlie bite the rebuke down and set about adding oats to a bucket as Jess clamps the edge of the bucket in her mouth and throws it aside. 'Jess!' Charlie snaps. 'I'm too tired for this.'

'Do you want it back?' Danny asks, picking it up.

'It's broken, Danny!'

'Sorry, I didn't see.'

'You didn't see the big crack in the side?'

'It's not Danny's fault,' Tappy says, grabbing another bucket to throw over at Charlie.

'Why don't I mix the feed, and you occupy Jess,' Henry says.

'I'm fine. I can do it.'

'Of course, you can, but many hands make light work.'

'Jess! I am not playing with you!'

I look over, thinking Jess doesn't look like she's playing either.

'I think she's just hungry,' I say, and something in my tone checks Charlie. She blinks for a second then nods quickly, and turns back, and I see her draw a deep breath, and when she next speaks, her voice is softer, and she reaches up to rub Jess's neck. Soothing the horse who stops throwing her head around and gently butts into Charlie while Henry pours oats into a new bucket.

'I'm sorry,' I hear Charlie whispering and push her head into Jess while discreetly wiping tears away.

'I'm sorry too,' Paula says, going over to wrap an arm around Charlie as the horse nestles into them both while Henry unscrews the lid from a big bottle of mineral water to pour into the bucket to mix with the oats. Not that he needed to with this rain coming down. Five minutes in the open would fill it with enough water.

'I'm sorry, Danny,' Charlie calls, looking over at the two lads near enough flaked out in the back of the Saxon, while Mads and Booker stand in the lee of the feed store watching everyone else.

'No harm. No foul,' Frank says. His legs planted, and his rifle held ready across his chest. 'You boys are alright though, aren't you,' he says to Danny and Mo. 'You did well today. Goods lads. Both of you. But stay switched on, cos we've got a bit more work to do yet. Come on. On your feet. I know it feels shitty when you're tired, but me and Carmen did 72 hours without sleep in Yemen. You remember that, Carmen?'

'I do.'

'You think that's bad? The lads in the trenches in the First World War did weeks with hardly any sleep and eating biscuits crawling with maggots. Point is, we train, and we stay fit, so when it gets hard, like it is now, we can endure. Eh? That's what winning is. It's enduring and getting back up more times than the other fucker. That's it. On your feet. Heads up. Get your feet planted in the ease position. You can stand for hours like this. Just gotta build up the stamina for it. See. Look the part, and you'll feel the part.'

They all respond, and I notice even Marcy stops leaning inside the doorway of the feed store and stands up straight.

'I think we're ready,' Henry says, showing Charlie who nods as Jess shoves her nose in to start munching quickly.

We drink bottled water, and I notice Carmen fussing over Reginald inside the feed store. 'Does it hurt?' she asks him.

'Not as much as I was anticipating,' he replies and, in

that one short sentence, sums up every injury we've had. That they hurt like hell, but not quite as much as they should. 'And therein lies the folly of our endeavour,' Reginald continues with his strong voice carrying clear to us all. 'Here we are, fighting the very thing keeping us alive.'

'We're not fighting the same thing that we have,' I call over.

'I think science would respectfully disagree,' Reginald says.

'I think science can fuck off,' I tell him.

'I shall pass that on, Mr Howie.'

'*We* are not evil,' Clarence says.

'Correction. We are not evil to our kind,' Henry says. 'Apart from Donna and Jim, of course.'

'We're not them,' I say.

'We are not who? The infected or Donna and Jim?' he asks.

'We're not the infected!' I snap.

'And yet,' Reginald says, holding his injured hand up.

'Don't even think it,' I tell him and everyone else. 'Don't let it into your heads. We're not them.'

'We're not exactly human anymore though,' Paula calls.

'We are not the infected,' I say.

'Saying it may not make it so,' Reginald says gently.

'How about the children it sent against us, or the heads it threw at us in the car park that day. Or what it did to my sister. Or Tucker and Jamie, and Curtis. How about what it did to Darren? Or Big Chris and Malcolm, and Blinky, and Joanie.'

'Blinky and Joanie didn't die from the infection,' Reginald says.

'They died because the infection exists!' I say in a rising tone.

'A tragedy, Mr Howie, but it doesn't counter the almost certain eventuality that we are the same as the thing we are fighting!'

'We are not them!'

'We have the same thing!'

'That doesn't make us the same!'

'How does it not?'

'Day two! A little boy in pyjamas, holding a teddy with blood all over his face.'

'I've seen the same carnage as you, Howie! But the fact remains we have the same thing inside of us.'

'We are not the fucking same! Day eighteen, Reginald. Day fucking eighteen. You heard it.'

'Heard what?' Carmen asks as the dark energy in my team spikes.

'The square. The little girl screaming for her mummy. Tell me we're the same. TELL ME WE ARE THE FUCKING SAME AS THAT.'

'Enough, Howie,' Paula calls, sagging against a wall to rub her face as Reginald glares at me then finally looks away.

'No,' he says quietly. 'No. We are not.'

'We're not the fucking same. We will never be the same. Get that out of your fucking heads. What we have is different. And yes, we might not be as human as we were, but we are not them. Do not humanise what they do.'

'No. No, of course,' Reginald says. 'We must maintain a clear separation. Mr Howie is right. We are not them.'

We stand in a heavy, awkward silence as the rain lashes down, and Jess eats the oats, and it's only then that I realise Meredith is pushing into my side. Her ears down, and her big eyes staring up at me in a way that makes me feel told off for shouting at her pack.

'I'm going for a piss,' I say and start heading over the road to a house with an open door. 'I'm fine, Dave. Stay here. I've got Meredith.'

Dave hesitates as though unsure but then concedes the order, and takes over my position in the road as I go in through another broken white UPVC door to the inside of another normal house with laminate flooring and pictures of people that are now dead on the walls. A small living room. A tiny dining room. A kitchen at the back. Every house the same. Every town the same. Every road. Every garden. Every set of curtains. Every set of utensils in pots or hanging from hooks, or stuff in drawers. Every washing up bowl. Every drainer, and I stand in the kitchen the same as all the others, glowering at it all and hating everything about it and the people we are trying to save.

The way we lived our lives, without proper freedom or proper thought.

I was the same. I worked at Tesco and earned my wages to buy a sofa and a TV, so on the days I wasn't working, I could eat the same food we sold and watch other humans on telly doing the same shitty, boring, arsewanking, mindless crap I was doing.

I rub my face while the rainwater pours off my body onto the crappy, laminated floor in the crappy house while thinking our old lives seem so dire and awful now.

But the most fucked up thing is that even now, if this infection suddenly stopped and the people that had it somehow recovered – we'd all go back to how we were within a few months.

So what's the fucking point then?

And that Donna and Jim. In my head, they represent the entirety of humanity, and suddenly, it all becomes confusing with the brief argument with Reginald and the idiot survivors of Rye, and all the other people we've saved all merging into one confusing clump of hatred.

I sag against the wall and spot an ashtray on the drainer. And where there's an ashtray…

I find rolling tobacco and cigarette papers on the small dining table, no doubt bought from Argos, because that's where everyone bought furniture from. Or Ikea. Or from catalogues back in the day. Or maybe Laura Ashley if they had a few quid.

I just about roll one up with a menthol filter and light it up with a satisfied groan.

I'll have this and go for a pee, and let the others come in, and have a moment out of the rain. I turn for the toilet and stop with a sad groan at the sight of the tropical fish tank on the side, and the once bright and vibrant fish floating on the top. The power must have gone out which stopped pumping air in, or they died of starvation.

Then I groan again at the rodent cage on the other side of the gas fireplace and wince at the sight of the dead hamster inside. The small water bottle empty. The small food bowl the same, and the hatred spikes again inside. The hatred for people. For the selfishness we had that made us trap and cage creatures for our pleasure without any thought to their welfare should we ever perish. Because how could we ever perish? We are people. We are the supreme beings of all creation and life.

'Fucking cunts,' I mutter, earning a look from Meredith as I head out of the living room and figure the house is too small for a downstairs toilet. I start up the stairs with the ciggy in my mouth and feel no such sense of pity for the dead body slowly liquidising into the stair carpet halfway up. An old lady, or maybe a young lady. She's too decomposed to tell. Could even be a man in female clothes. No judgment here. All people are cunts, regardless of how they identify.

I reach the top and aim for the bathroom.

A scratch.

A tiny whimper.

I turn fast as Meredith scrabbles up the stairs. I slam into a closed bedroom door and wilt back from the smell of death inside. Gagging and retching, and covering my mouth as my eyes take in a cot on the side, and the dead body of a baby inside.

I turn away from the sight then cry out at the golden Labrador dog on her side, and her pups gathered in around her teats. All of them dead. The mother dog's ribs poking out from hunger. The pups the same.

A yell out in anguish at the sight.

A scratch.

A tiny whimper.

A puppy moves.

'ROY!' I scream out and drop to my knees, then force my movements to go slower as I gently lift the puppy. Feeling the horrifying lack of weight in its emaciated body. 'ROY!' I shout again as the puppy labours for air to the sound of feet bursting through the door and mounting the stairs as the puppy exhales but doesn't inhale. 'No... nonononono!'

'What?' Roy gasps, bursting into the room with Dave and rushing to the baby.

'Come on... Please,' I say as Roy turns and lurches over to me. 'Do something.'

'Do what?' he asks me as I thrust the puppy at him.

'It was alive.'

'What's happening?' Paula asks, pushing into the room.

'Oh god. Is that...' she cuts off, checking the baby then seeing the puppy in Roy's hands.

'It was alive,' I tell them.

'It's not now, Howie,' he says.

'Make it live! Do something,' I say with tears streaming down my cheeks as Marcy and Henry get to the door with Clarence behind them. 'Do something, Roy!'

'I'm not a vet, Howie!'

'Let me,' Carmen says, pushing in to take the puppy in her hands. 'Hold its head for me,' she orders, with Marcy taking the puppy's tiny head to hold with trembling hands as Carmen opens the mouth and blows in gently while massaging the ribs.

'Please,' I say, whispering the words out. Wishing with every ounce of my being for that puppy to live. Praying to any God listening to just do this one thing. To give this one life back. From all the carnage. From all the misery. From all the pain and suffering. Just this one life.

'Come on,' Marcy says, her voice cracking with emotion as the tears pour down Clarence's cheeks, and Carmen blows into the lungs and massages the chest.

'Maybe try some water?' Paula suggests. 'It's so dry in here.' She runs her hand over her beret to soak it and puts the tip of her finger into the puppy's mouth.

'Don't drown it,' Roy says.

'Sorry!' Paula says, pulling back in panic. 'I didn't think. Come on. Breathe little one...'

'Just take a breath,' Marcy whispers, and Carmen exhales into the puppy's mouth as the hope shines down that we can do this one thing. That from all this horror and badness we can save one innocent life. It will happen. It has to happen because surely no God can ever be that cruel.

And yet.

And yet.

And yet.

I sink onto my haunches as Carmen slows down with her own tears pouring down her cheeks, and Marcy's lip trembling as we realise nothing we can do will bring the life back into the puppy in her hands.

It hits me hard.

It hits me harder than anything I have ever felt in my life.

Rage.

And I'm up and out. Pushing through them and into the bathroom to stand shaking from head to toe, and in the mirror, I see my eyes turning red, and that rage inside wants to destroy and kill, and tear everything apart.

It was still alive.

It lasted a month.

Why?

Why do that to us?

I feel so angry. So very, very angry, and for a split second, I visualise tearing the house apart with my bare hands.

But I don't.

I go back out and see the others where I left them.

I take the puppy from Marcy's hands and place the body with the others, and scoop them all up into a blanket. 'Take the mother,' I whisper. 'Get the mother!' I snap when nobody moves. Someone picks her up. I don't know who, and we all go downstairs, and we all go outside into the garden into the rain, and I lower down onto my knees and draw my knife, and stab the ground to start making a hole.

Henry finds a trowel. Marcy finds a fork. We all use something and dig down into the mud as the rain pelts down until the hole is deep and wide.

We put the mother dog in first then the pups with her. It breaks me inside. Like when we buried Blinky. Like that.

We cover them with soil. We don't speak. What could we say?

We don't give a prayer either.

I hate God.

I hate God as much as I hate people.

With everything I have.

With every ounce of my existence.

And when we stand back, I feel that hatred burning inside.

And when we go back to the vehicles, I look at Reginald and for the first time since this started, I truly think we should just let the infection win.

14

Day Thirty
Saturday
The Fat Bee Garden Centre

A narrow road bordered by thick hedges leads to a long car park, enclosed by high metal fences topped with razor wire.

We get inside to see the garden centre is built on a hill with a basement level below the ground floor level next to us. A large parking area. Sheds and log cabins, and greenhouses on display off to one side.

A metal roller cage covers the front doors. We use the chains attached to the Saxon to wrench them away, then Carmen breaks the lock.

We should be done. We should be able to rest.

Except we can't.

And what comes next is fucking gruelling because while the battle might be over, the work certainly isn't.

'Sergeant Blowers, take your squad and check the perimeter,' Henry orders. I stay silent. Recalling our discussion about Henry taking the lead with this stuff. 'Look for breaks or weak points, and points of access.'

'Yes, Major,' Blowers says, nodding in his pink beret for his team to move over to the side with him.

'That leaves us to do the inside,' Henry says. 'Dave, you take point. Carmen, you take the rear. We check every room as we go through. Clear?'

Dave takes the lead, or rather, Meredith takes the actual lead and powers on ahead of us with her nose to the ground.

'Hold,' Henry whispers in the foyer. 'Howie. Your experience counts here. What's your instincts telling you?'

'Air is stale,' I reply quietly. 'Dust on the sides and floor.'

A quick nod from Henry, then he gives a single tap to Dave, and we're off, with Dave sweeping behind the customer returns desk to what looks like an admin office connected to a manager's office, but with decent windows overlooking the car park and the road in.

Henry motions to Bash then points to his own eyes before patting the air with the flat of his hand then pointing to the car park and front. *Stay here. Eyes on.*

Bash nods, taking position by the window as Dave sweeps out, and we breach into the garden centre proper. A wide aisle bordered by hundreds of indoor plants on display in tiers, creating a lush, green environment rich with oxygen, and with the rain hitting the metal roof, it feels almost tropical.

We reach an intersection.

The café off to the right. A much larger area off to the left, with shelves and display units selling all manner of garden and outdoor things. A wide metal staircase ahead of us leading to the warehouse style vast shopping area below.

Dave pauses. Waiting instruction. Henry motions his eyes to Marcy then pats the air.

You stay here. Watch the front. Watch the sides. Watch the stairs.

Marcy nods and takes position as Henry motions for Dave to go right, and we sweep into the canteen. Plain wooden tables and chairs. Nothing fancy. Nothing posh. I like it instantly.

A counter to the left. Chalkboard menus offering full English breakfasts. Sandwiches and toasties. Baguettes. Jacket potatoes. My mouth waters. My belly rumbles. I'm not the only one. I'd sacrifice a toe right now for a ham and cheese toastie.

We get into the kitchen. A sea of stainless steel. Spotless save for the dust, which is a good sign.

What's also a good sign are the pantries and storage rooms, and the well-insulated walk-in fridge which hasn't built up a high internal temperature. Trays of eggs and airtight sealed packets of bacon and sausages, and steaks, and chicken breasts.

We go back to Marcy, with Henry motioning for her to hold position while we check the other side. Ranging out with rifles up.

All clear.

We go down the stairs into the darker warehouse area and pause to let our eyes adjust to the dark. But from the musty smell of the air and the thick dust, and the lack of reaction from Meredith, I get the sense this place hasn't been touched since it all started.

But complacency kills, so we keep our focus up and sweep through the outdoor camping supply area. Tents. Sleeping bags. Folding chairs. Racks of outdoor clothing and boots. Then we pass through the displays of garden furniture and shelves filled with garden lights, and on to an area selling home furniture. Beds and bedding. A few dining tables. A few sofas.

We reach the end, and I think that's it, but Henry shakes his head and points to the wall, and it takes me a second or two to realise it's not a wall, but a triple width rolling metal shutter.

A set of green and red buttons on the side, but no power. Paula nudges Clarence and points up to a hanging chain on a loop. A nod from Henry. Clarence grips it with his one good hand and starts feeding it on the loop, with the metal shutter opening instantly on well-oiled hinges.

A big workshop and vehicle loading area greets us on the other side. Big enough for three vans in a row. Only one sits there now next to a forklift truck.

We sweep in and check the staffroom and staff toilets, and a few more storerooms, and cleaning cupboards.

'Another chain,' Clarence says quietly as we look to the external wall and another triple sized metal shutter.

Henry nods. The big man winches it open, with us pointing rifles out to Blowers, and his team pointing rifles in at us.

'Told you they'd open it,' Tappy says, getting a fist bump from Maddox. 'And hello,' she adds at the workshop and the many tools on the wall, and the Snap On tool chests, and workbenches. 'Nick. We've found our forever home.'

A few tired snorts. A slight lessening of the heightened sense.

'Fence line is good. No breaks. No signs of entry,' Blowers relays.

'Excellent work, Sergeant,' Henry says. 'Tappy, bring our vehicles down the ramp and inside. We'll use the workshop area to strip and clean the weapons. Sergeant, Bash is on watch. Organise a rota. I don't want anyone on stag for more than thirty minutes at a time. We're too tired so the risk of falling asleep is high. And I think, most importantly, we need to get a brew on. Suggest we rig something up in here for now. We're dripping filthy water, so let's try and contain ourselves to this area until we've got cleaned up. Any questions?'

'Does Marcy need to stay where she is?' Paula asks.

'No, she's clear to stand down. We'll assess the sentry position later, but for now, the admin office will suffice. Right. Let's get this done, and then we can R&R.'

It was the right decision letting Henry take the lead.

※ ※

We set to work, with Tappy and Mads driving the Saxon and the Royal Mail van down the ramp while Booker takes the Fat Bee Garden Centre delivery van outside to make room, while Nick finds a generator and gets it going to rig lights up inside the workshop.

That's while Paula takes camping gas stoves off the shelves and gets them going to heat water for a brew while everyone else organises areas to work in while minimising our contact with the inside areas. We're covered in shit. I can even see chunks of roasted, crispy human flesh stuck in the laces of my boots.

We get to work stripping rifles. Cleaning and oiling them through. Checking the moving parts. Clearing the bits of flesh and skin away and reloading magazines with the limited supplies of ammunitions we have left.

'Okay! Brew's up!' Paula calls to a tired but very appreciative groan as we grab mugs of tea and take five. Our clothes still drenched. Our hands dirty with oil and grease.

Our bodies hurt and wrapped in gaffer tape. Paula and Marcy take the brews up for Danny and Mo on sentry and come back with packets of biscuits.

We drink tea and munch through several packets. Jess and Meredith in the workshop, with Charlie taking the bales of straw she got from the feed place to make an area for Jess to one end.

After a brew, we do sidearms. Clean. Check. Oil. Reload. Make ready.

When that's done, we start on the vehicles.

We focus on the Saxon. Spraying everything inside with anti-bac and then hosing it out. Everyone does something. Dave puts new edges on blades.

We don't speak while we work, other than simple requests to pass this or move that.

We don't joke.

We don't banter.

The puppy died, and the poor horses stay locked in until they perished from thirst and starvation.

I hate God.

I hate people.

There's no humour in any of us.

Even Paula works in silence. Marcy. Carmen.

Neither Frank nor Cookey make quips.

Then it's done. The weapons. The vehicles.

Now it's us that need cleaning.

'There's a single staff shower,' Paula says with a shrug. 'Or outside,' she adds as we look to the torrential rain coming down through the open rolling shutter doors. 'It's not cold,' she says.

Paula takes Carmen, Marcy, Charlie, and Tappy around the back of one of the outbuildings while we go down the side of the garden centre and strip down, and scrub our bodies with whatever soap and gel Paula found inside.

We don't speak or joke.

We each find a spot away from the others and scrub our naked bodies in the rain, and the water around our feet runs black and red from the filth and blood.

I still feel hot inside. Like my insides are baked. It was that heat. That was something else. I don't think I'll ever truly feel cool or even cold again.

We stand in silence for a very long time under the rain.

I think about the puppy. I can't stop thinking about the puppy.

I hate the owner of that house.

Maybe it was her on the stairs.

I'm glad she's dead.

I hate her.

※ ※

We stay outside in the rain for a long time.

We dry off using new towels coated in chemicals that don't do anything, and we get dressed in new clothes taken from the outdoor clothing section inside the garden centre. All of it mass-produced by children or people trapped in poverty in third-world countries while Donna stuffed her fat face, and Jim tugged his penis while watching internet porn, and the lady in that house fed her caged fish and caged hamster, and bred her beautiful golden Labrador.

Was that her baby in the cot?

I don't know.

I don't care.

The puppy died.

Our old clothes are bagged and secured to one side. Our

boots hosed and sprayed, and scrubbed, and hosed again, then stacked inside to dry.

Everything takes time. And energy.

Energy we don't have.

But eventually, even we get cleaned and finally head inside the Garden Centre and up the metal stairs to the canteen where we open tins and pour food into big metal pans that get heated on gas stoves for Paula's Special Stew, while Nick and Tappy find another genny to get power into the coffee machine.

We notice the inside of the café is dark from the low clouds, so we take a few battery-operated lanterns from the shelves to put on.

We drink bottled water.

We drag tables together in the café area.

We don't speak.

We don't joke.

We carry the big metal pans out, and we each take a bowl and spoon food in, and find a spot to eat.

We eat in silence.

When the first big pan runs out, we bring the other big pan out, and we eat in silence.

After eating, Meredith lies down on her side. Scrubbed. Dried, and full.

I notice Jess clip clopping into the café and get up to pour oat milk into a bucket before she trashes the place.

'Go and sleep,' I tell the others and pick my rifle up. 'I'll take first watch.'

I go to the front door and spot Nick's battered packet of smokes on the side by the customer returns desk, and light one up while using my foot to hold the front door open an inch to blow the smoke out.

Later, Marcy comes out to join me with a mug of hot tea. I'd have preferred coffee. I don't say anything. She doesn't either. We sit in folding camping chairs, with our rifles within reach, and stare out the glass doors to the rain outside.

I hate God.

I hate people.

I hate them so much I want to do something terrible.

'Shush,' Marcy says quietly and reaches over to take my hand in hers. She's crying. I cry too. The puppy. It's broken me.

'Me too,' she whispers.

We sit still for a long time.

'Maybe Cassie was right,' I whisper.

She doesn't say anything for a long time. I hear her swallow and wipe her cheeks.

'Your eyes went very red,' she whispers.

I don't know what that means.

We hold hands, and we sit in silence.

Filled with hatred.

When it starts growing dark, Marcy slips away and comes back with two mugs of tea and several packets of biscuits.

The sight of Meredith and Jess following Marcy into the foyer then into the admin office would normally make me smile. It doesn't now.

Clarence comes in and grunts a thank you to Marcy for making the tea and getting the biscuits.

'How's the hand?' I ask, noticing the gaffer tape has been replaced with a bandage, held in place with fresh tape.

'It's not growing back if that's what you mean.'

I snort a dry laugh just to give a response.

'Roy checked us all over,' he tells us both. 'He said he couldn't stitch anyone because the skin had already started scabbing. He said we need to let the infection work.'

I share a look with Marcy.

We head downstairs and through the barbeque sections, and outdoor seating displays, and all the sorts of things mass produced and shipped over in emission-spewing ships, so that Donna and Jim could come and get triggered by the high prices, and stuff their already fat faces with scones and fried food in the canteen.

'This is ours,' Marcy whispers, leading us to a double bed. I don't question why there is a double bed in a garden centre.

I nod and strip down, and keep my boots and trousers, and rifle, and axe all within easy reach. Then we get onto the bed. We don't get in. It's too hot. We lie in the near darkness, listening to the rain on the metal roof above us, and I hear the snores of the others nearby.

Marcy exhales and rolls into my side.

For a second, I think she'll start whispering things.

She doesn't.

I lay there for a long time with that hatred inside. But it's not the hatred I had before that made me want to kill the infected.

This is different.

Very different.

In the foyer, Clarence exhales a long blast of air through his nose and stands close to the doors, listening to the rain pelting the concrete surface of the car park. His eyes adjusting to the dark.

He also knows this rain is so heavy even a bloodhound couldn't track them.

A nudge in the back from Jess. He turns, spotting Meredith sitting by the customer returns desk, staring longingly at the packets of biscuits.

He goes over and picks the custard creams up with his left hand, and brings his right hand up to cinch the wrapper.

Except he doesn't have a right hand.

'Bugger,' he mutters as Paula reaches past him to cinch the end with her right hand.

'Hold it,' she whispers.

He holds too hard. She pulls too hard, and the custard creams fall out, with Meredith and Jess lunging to gobble them up.

'Sorry,' Clarence whispers.

'It's okay. We'll learn together,' Paula says and slides her backside on the returns desk, and lifts her tea to sip while Clarence stands a little awkwardly. A man of immense strength and ability, but one prone to great nerves at the merest hint of romance.

She reaches out to guide him in closer and rests her head on his chest. They don't move for a long time.

Both thinking of the same thing.

The puppy.

It broke all of them.

What it meant.

What it represented.

Donna. Jim.

People.

The infection.

What Reginald said about fighting the thing keeping them alive.

The fort. All the troubles there.

Joanie.

Blinky.

The survivors in Gatwick, and how fucking hard it was to make them move and keep them alive.

The survivors everywhere else, and how fucking hard it is to ever make them move and keep them alive.

But that puppy.

That was too much.

                        🙦 🙤

The same disquiet and disharmony is felt by all of them.

But maybe not all for the same reasons, and Major Henry Campbell-Dillington, formerly of the Parachute Regiment, and then of the Special Air Service, which was before he *disappeared* into the shadowy world of the intelligence and security services where he honed skills of perception over a lifetime of work on the very front line of combat and espionage.

And even after the day before with Gatwick and then this morning with Camber and Rye, that mind processing those perceptions hasn't turned off. Nor did it *during* the days before, or within the fighting and while in transit between locations. Or even when he had a rushed conversation in the pouring rain when he clocked the eyelines of the others and how they lingered.

Now he sits on the edge of his bed, watching the metal staircase. The low light casting his features in harsh shadows.

Motion. Someone moving around. Reginald watches

quietly as the figure goes up the stairs almost silently. Reginald follows a second later. Rising up the stairs and slipping silently into the men's toilets to see one of the cubicle doors closed. A rustle of clothing comes from inside the cubicle. Then another sound. A rushed noise of skin moving fast on skin, but slightly wet, followed by an almost silent grunt.

Reginald frowns and slips back out and over to the dark shadows in the canteen to watch the person coming out while figuring it's not uncommon for young men to masturbate. Stress is a real thing that manifests in all sorts of different ways, and it's also true that masturbation provides a fast hit of endorphins and a quick release of pressure. So that act alone is not one which causes concern.

Except it's not that act alone, and although he can't prove a thing, nor does he have anything firm to go on at all, something just doesn't sit right.

And the last thing they need right now, straight after Gatwick, and after Rye, and after the whole damnable, rotten puppy thing is another drama developing.

But then, a strong counter argument would suggest *that surely isn't better to deal with it now, instead of something potentially exploding later at completely the wrong time?*

Which, of course, is entirely correct, and if this rain is here for a few days, then this might be a good opportunity.

Reginald sits in the shadows of the canteen and watches the young man slip out of the toilet and head downstairs.

'So be it then,' Reginald whispers to himself. 'For the good of the pack.'

15

Gentle mist on my face.

I start falling, but everywhere around me is grey, until I spot the churning sea beneath me. I don't who I am. I don't even know my name.

I scream in terror because everyone knows if you die in a dream, you die for real, and I know deep inside that I'll wake up before I hit the surface.

Except, that doesn't happen.

I hit the surface and plunge deep into the black waters, and kick, and thrash, and my lungs fill with water, and my mind blacks out.

Awake.

Gasping.

'My name is Howie!' I cry out, knowing who I am. Knowing my name, and for a split-second, I think I've woken in my bed in the Garden Centre, but then I realise I'm still dreaming, because I'm in the other place.

The place I went to when I died.

The broken world with the playpark that's all rusty, and the buildings all around me are nothing more than rubble, and when I look up, the sky is torn and the colour of blood.

But why am I here?

Am I dead?

'I have got a night off... I have got a night off.'

A singsong voice that I recognise with a sickening jolt of familiarity, because it's my voice. Except I'm not singing. The other Howie is. The one that just walked past me and sat down on my sofa to watch my TV in my old flat in Boroughfare - except the sofa and the TV are slap bang in the middle of the apocalyptic street.

He's even got my coffee table and the pizza box on the top of it, and I watch while experiencing some form of weird, fucked up, out-of-body, time-travel dream experience.

The other me looks so different though. He's all pale, with a little belly on him, and not a bite or a scratch on him.

'Must be something on,' the me on the sofa mumbles while flicking through the channels.

I can't take my eyes off him.

'And we're getting reports of large-scale riots and disorder across multiple European cities...'

It won't be long until I'll start recognising the places they are talking about as the outbreak spreads across central and then western Europe.

Then the channels will stop transmitting.

The phones will go down.

And I'll hear the big guy from the pizza shop being chased outside. I'll even go out and try, and help, but I'll be too late, and I'll come back inside here and barricade the doors.

That's nuts.

If it was now, I'd run out of my garden gate and attack

the infected with my bare hands, and bite their fucking throats out.

'The transformation in you in such a short time is remarkable, Howie.'

I turn to see a woman sitting at a plain wooden table staring at me intensely. 'Come, sit with me. We don't have long,' she says and motions the other chair. I turn to glance at the other me on the sofa as Clarence walks by with his top off and big boobs like Marcy. 'Anything on, Boss?' he asks and sits down next to the other me and takes a slice of pizza.

'Howie,' the woman says, bringing my attention back to her motioning to the other chair. 'Sit. We don't have long.'

'What the fuck,' I say and shake my head to wake up.

'This isn't a dream, Howie. That is, but this is not,' the woman says, nodding past me to the other me on the sofa next to the big-boobed topless Clarence. 'Your mind is creating those images and merging them with this reality.'

'Who are you?'

'I am known as the Old Lady.'

I frown at her name. Thinking she only looks about fifty, with brown hair streaked with grey. Attractive too. But like a CEO or the headteacher of a posh school. A plain, white shirt with the top few buttons undone and the sleeves rolled up. Tight, blue denim jeans and casual boots. Casual but smart at the same time.

'Ah, Mr Howie,' Reginald says from the window next to the sofa which just appeared because there definitely wasn't a window there a second ago, not that it's an actual window either, but just an empty wooden frame that Reginald is peering through in that intellectual way he does. 'We need to observe the other player in case they are putting pineapple on their pizza,' he says and turns to show me his big boobs that start bouncing when he slaps his fly swatter on his thigh. 'Pineapples, Mr Howie!'

'Why have they all got big boobs?'

'Don't read anything into it,' the Old Lady says. 'Dreams don't mean anything, contrary to some apparent experts. Come. Sit. Focus on me.'

I sit down and stare at her, and my chest lurches with a sudden pain as she leans closer to rest her arms on the table. 'My chest,' I say with a wince while rubbing at it.

'That's your body bringing you back to life. You are awfully hard to kill, Howie. Shush. Listen. There are multiple worlds which Freedom want to destroy.'

'Who?'

'My task is to make sure as many worlds as possible reach the end.'

'The end of what?'

'The end of the beginning.'

'Eh!?'

'The period your world was in before the outbreak later comes to be known as The Age Of Wrath. Many worlds go through that period, but only yours suffers this outbreak. But, if a world can get through that period and into The Age Of Enlightenment, it will connect to the other worlds, and life becomes very different. It becomes a utopia where all things exist in harmony, without disease or suffering. Don't interrupt. I am from Discovery. We seek survival. But every up has a down. Every right has a wrong. Every force *must* have an opposing force. There is another force out there called Freedom, who seek only chaos and disorder, and right now, your world has gone suddenly very dark, and I very much fear they have turned you away from the path.'

'What path?' I say, not getting a word as the world around me turns black and starts filling with glowing, golden lines. Just a few at first, seeming to grow as they stretch out, but it's like we're moving with them, and they multiply fast. Becoming dozens then hundreds, then thousands, then hundreds of thousands, and more, and more, and many more, until it feels as if we've shrunk to tiny dots, and we're seeing something on an unimaginable scale. Millions. Billions. Trillions of lines, all crossing each other with tiny pulsing dots at key points.

'That was your world,' she says, with her voice seeming to float around me. 'Each glowing line represents a life, and each glowing orb represents a pivotal change in their life, or an access point that can be used to influence the timelines.' I realise *all of the lines* are still moving and growing, and expanding, until every single line runs into one huge, pulsing, glowing, golden dot.

'And that big one is the outbreak,' her voice says, and I frown, still not having a clue what she means. But then I notice that very few golden lines come out of the golden dots, and only a fraction of what was before.

'Nearly ten billion lives before the outbreak, and now your world is down to just a few million, and thousands are dying each day at a rate your world cannot sustain. But we had hope, Howie. We knew you'd punch through. And then, this happened,' she says as nearly all of the golden lines fade away and become indistinct and blurred.

'What is that?'

'That is what happened when you found the dying puppy. I sent Bear and Thomas to observe.'

'Who are-.'

'Operatives. It doesn't matter. What matters is that you are wavering,' she says in a harder voice as the lines and the blackness seem to dissolve, until we're back to normal, and I'm staring over the table at her intense brown eyes fixed on me. Her hand still rests on the table, but she leans in and lifts her index finger to point at me. 'Finding the dying puppy was a rotten thing that represents the suffering and the feelings of inadequacy you all feel at trying to fight such overwhelming numbers while it feels like every survivor you meet seems entitled and greedy and ultimately unworthy. I understand why that would affect you. But you cannot stop now. You don't see the good you are doing.'

'Who the fuck are you? Are you the infection?' I ask, feeling my own eyes harden as I consider the possibility that the infection, which is inside of me, has somehow awoken and is trying to communicate. I start to rise. Seeing it right in front of me, and woman or not, I'll rip its fucking throat out.

A scrape of a shoe sounds out as though someone pushed off to come at us, but she lifts a hand. Telling whoever it is to stop as I catch sight of a tall, lean man with a deep-set eyes and brooding expression before he slips back into the shadows.

'Why would the infection tell you to keep fighting?' she asks.

'Then, who are you?'

'I am not a who. I'm a system. An entity. It's complicated, and I really do not have the time to explain. I'm breaking rules by doing this.'

'By doing what?'

'Well, having Bear spray a certain substance in your face while you sleep to stop your heart and cause temporary death is one of them. You'll be fine. As I said. You are very hard to kill.'

'This is nuts. I need to wake up.' I clench my fists and will myself to wake as I feel a funny lurch in my chest. 'What was that?'

'That's the infection not letting you die,' she says quickly, leaning over the table. 'Look at me. Look at me! You cannot stop. Howie!'

My chest lurches again, like my heart is misfiring or beating wrong.

'You have to fight, Howie.'

'I don't want to fight!'

'You must! Or the infection wins.'

'It wins anyway. Reggie said we can't save people. The panacea *is* the infection. Humans are done.'

'Your version must survive, Howie. That panacea is what every world gains in the far future. But it is a product of evolution that takes thousands of years to happen, and only after devastating wars take place that alter the genetic coding within people. But Freedom found a way to extract it and turn it into the infection, and they released it into your world.'

'I don't get any of this, and I don't fucking care. Fuck the infection, and fuck freedom. This is just a dream. Argh! Shit, my chest!'

'You don't see the good you are doing, Howie! If the other side wins, this world is lost. You must fight.'

'Fuck you!'

'You will fight,' she says and reaches out to grip my chin, and comes in close as though she can see all the way into my very soul. I try shake my head, but she's as strong as Clarence. 'I am showing you the path and you *will* keep going. You *will* fight. Or I will take what you love and I will cut this world off.'

I fly backwards out of her grip and sit up in bed, rubbing at my chest while listening to the rain on the metal roof of the garden centre.

'You okay?' Marcy asks sleepily, rolling onto her back in

a bra as I look at her boobs in the light from the low-glow lantern and suddenly remember Clarence and Reginald from my dream.

'Had a messed-up dream,' I murmur and rub my face that feels wet, and when I pull my hands away, I can smell something. 'What is that?' I ask in alarm.

'What?' she asks, coming awake with a concerned look and taking my hands to sniff.

'I think a bear tried to kill me.'

'What bear? That's the hibiscrub, you idiot. The hibiscrub? The medical soap Roy put out for us? Smell my hands... They're the same.'

I sniff her hands then my own with that chemical or somewhat medical aroma on both.

'Come on, lie down,' she says and pulls me down to her side, and runs her fingertips over my forehead and cheek. 'Everything is fine,' she whispers sleepily as I listen to the rain on the roof and start sliding back into sleep. My mind once more fills with weird images of a big boobed Clarence eating my pizza and getting told off by Reginald because it's got pineapple on it.

I don't know why though.

I like pineapple on pizza.

ALSO BY RR HAYWOOD

Washington Post, Wall Street Journal, Amazon & Audible bestselling author, RR Haywood. One of the most downloaded indie authors in the UK with nearly four million books sold and over 25 Kindle bestsellers.

DELIO. PHASE ONE

*WINNER OF "*BEST NEW BOOK*" DISCOVER SCI-FI 2023

#1 Amazon & Audible bestseller

A single bed in a small room.

The centre of Piccadilly Circus.

A street in New York city outside of a 7-Eleven.

A young woman taken from her country.

A drug dealer who paid his debt.

A suicidal, washed-up cop.

The rest of the world now frozen.

Unmoving.

Unblinking.

"Brilliant."

"A gripping story. Harrowing, and often hysterical."

"This book is very different to anything else out there - and brilliantly so."

"You'll fall so hard for these characters, you'll wish the world would freeze just so you could stay with them forever."

*

FICTION LAND

Nominated for Best Audio Book at the British Book Awards 2023

Narrated by Gethin Anthony

The #1 Most Requested Audio Book in the UK 2023

Now Optioned For A TV Series

#1 Amazon bestseller

#1 Audible bestseller

"Imagine John Wick wakes up in a city full of characters from novels – that's Fiction Land."

Not many men get to start over.

John Croker did and left his old life behind – until crooks stole his delivery van. No van means no pay, which means his niece doesn't get the life-saving operation she needs, and so in desperation, John uses the skills of his former life one last time… That is until he dies and wakes up in Fiction Land. A city occupied by characters from unfinished novels.

But the world around him doesn't feel right, and when he starts asking questions, the authorities soon take extreme measures to stop him finding the truth about Fiction Land.

*

EXTRACTED SERIES

EXTRACTED

EXECUTED

EXTINCT

Blockbuster Time-Travel

#1 Amazon US

#1 Amazon UK

#1 Audible US & UK

Washington Post & Wall Street Journal Bestseller

In 2061, a young scientist invents a time machine to fix a tragedy in his past. But his good intentions turn catastrophic when an early test reveals something unexpected: the end of the world.

A desperate plan is formed. Recruit three heroes, ordinary humans capable of extraordinary things, and change the future.

Safa Patel is an elite police officer, on duty when Downing Street comes under terrorist attack. As armed men storm through the breach, she dispatches them all.

'Mad' Harry Madden is a legend of the Second World War. Not only did he complete an impossible mission—to plant charges on a heavily defended submarine base—but he also escaped with his life.

Ben Ryder is just an insurance investigator. But as a young man he witnessed a gang assaulting a woman and her child. He went to their rescue, and killed all five.

Can these three heroes, extracted from their timelines at the point of death, save the world?

*

THE CODE SERIES

The Worldship Humility

The Elfor Drop

The Elfor One

#1 Audible bestselling smash hit narrated by Colin Morgan

#1 Amazon bestselling Science-Fiction

"A rollicking, action packed space adventure…"

"Best read of the year!"

"An original and exceptionally entertaining book."
"A beautifully written and humorous adventure."

Sam, an airlock operative, is bored. Living in space should be full of adventure, except it isn't, and he fills his time hacking 3-D movie posters.

Petty thief Yasmine Dufont grew up in the lawless lower levels of the ship, surrounded by violence and squalor, and now she wants out. She wants to escape to the luxury of the Ab-Spa, where they eat real food instead of rats and synth cubes.

Meanwhile, the sleek-hulled, unmanned Gagarin has come back from the ever-continuing search for a new home. Nearly all hope is lost that a new planet will ever be found, until the Gagarin returns with a code of information that suggests a habitable planet has been found. This news should be shared with the whole fleet, but a few rogue captains want to colonise it for themselves.

When Yasmine inadvertently steals the code, she and Sam become caught up in a dangerous game of murder, corruption, political wrangling and...porridge, with sex-addicted Detective Zhang Woo hot on their heels, his own life at risk if he fails to get the code back.

*

THE UNDEAD SERIES

THE UK's #1 Horror Series

Available on Amazon & Audible

"The Best Series Ever…"

The Undead. The First Seven Days

The Undead. The Second Week.

The Undead Day Fifteen.

The Undead Day Sixteen.

The Undead Day Seventeen

The Undead Day Eighteen

The Undead Day Nineteen

The Undead Day Twenty

The Undead Day Twenty-One

The Undead Twenty-Two

The Undead Twenty-Three: The Fort

The Undead Twenty-Four: Equilibrium

The Undead Twenty-Five: The Heat

The Undead Twenty-Six: Rye

Blood on the Floor
An Undead novel

Blood at the Premiere
An Undead novel

The Camping Shop
An Undead novella

*

A Town Called Discovery.

The #1 Amazon & Audible Time Travel Thriller

A man falls from the sky. He has no memory.

What lies ahead are a series of tests. Each more brutal than the last, and if he gets through them all, he might just reach A Town Called Discovery.

*

THE FOUR WORLDS OF BERTIE CAVENDISH

A rip-roaring multiverse time-travel crossover starring:

The Undead

Extracted.

A Town Called Discovery

and featuring

The Worldship Humility

*

www.rrhaywood.com

Find me on Facebook:

https://www.facebook.com/RRHaywood/

Find me on Twitter:

https://twitter.com/RRHaywood

Printed in Great Britain
by Amazon